I0763438

THE SCIENTISTS

A Clint Smith Thriller

Special Edition

FIRST EDITION

THE SCIENTISTS

A Clint Smith Thriller

Bob Doerr

TotalRecall Publications, Inc.
1103 Middlecreek
Friendswood, Texas 77546
281-992-3131
www.mousegate.com

ISBN: 978-1-64883-312-0
UPC: 6-43977-43120-2

Library of Congress Control Number: 2023945455

FIRST EDITION
1 2 3 4 5 6 7 8 9 10

To those who serve.

AND

TO RON AND SARAH

FOR DRAGGING ME AROUND GREECE.

Award Winning Author: Bob Doerr

grew up in a military family, graduated from the Air Force Academy, and had a career of his own in the Air Force. Bob specialized in criminal investigations and counterintelligence gaining significant insight to the worlds of crime, espionage, and terrorism. His work brought him into close coordination with the security agencies of many countries and filled his mind with the fascinating plots and characters found in his books today. His education credits include a Masters in International Relations from Creighton University. A full-time author with twenty published books and a co-author in another, Bob was selected by the Military Writers Society of America as its Author of the Year for 2013. The Eric Hoffer Awards awarded *No One Else to Kill* its 2013 first runner up to the grand prize for commercial fiction. Two of his other books were finalists for the Eric Hoffer Award in earlier contests. *Loose Ends Kill* won the 2011 Silver medal for Fiction/mystery by the Military Writers Society of America. *Another Colorado Kill* received the same Silver medal in 2012 and the silver medal for general fiction at the Branson Stars and Flags national book contest in 2012. Bob released *Double Bogeys Can Kill,* his ninth book in the Jim West mystery series, in 2022. Bob has also written four novellas for middle grade readers in his Enchanted Coin series: *The Enchanted Coin, The Rescue of Vincent, The Magic of Vex,* and *Stranded in Space*. Bob lives in Garden Ridge, Texas, with Leigh, his wife of 50 years, and Cinco, their ornery cat.

About the Book

This is the 5th Clint Smith novel. Clint is a hunter, a government assassin, employed by a very small, ultra secret agency. Someone has been kidnapping scientists from various countries. All are tops in their field and experts in the modernization of drones. As the world's security and intelligence services make little progress in solving the disappearances, Clint is put on alert. Three separate drone attacks occur, resulting in a number of deaths. Once the lethal drones are perfected, the kidnapped scientists' usefulness comes to an end. While Clint's mission does not include rescue, he's given the green light to go after his target. His success may prevent some of them from dying. Time is tight and the enemy is no pushover, but the game is on.

Chapter 1

Dr. Maurice Hockenberry walked out of the apartment, trying to make as little noise as possible. His wife and two young boys still slept soundly inside. The Spanish sunrise created brilliant shades of red to pink streaks in the clouds. He smelled the scent of the sea in the breeze.

A beautiful morning, he thought while he walked the hundred yards to the bakery. He knew the cooks there would already be busy making churros and other morning delights. An old woman dressed in the traditional black walked slowly on the other side of the street. He thought she was probably heading to the same destination. Other than the woman and a black cat that sat on top of a parked car, the streets appeared empty at this early hour.

At the bakery, he bought a dozen churros hot out of the fryer. The young lady at the counter smiled at him when he paid and passed a broken churro to him on a napkin.

"For you," she said. Her smile sent a little tingle through him.

"Thank you, I'm sure I'll be back later this week," he said, taking a bite of the broken churro as he stepped out onto the sidewalk.

He felt great. Life was good. His company had paid for his travel to Spain to attend the three-day international conference on the "Pragmatic Future of Drones." He loved the topic. While he had an engineering degree from Purdue, his Doctorate had focused on "Drones: Destroyers or Saviors".

The wide variety of presentations and papers handed out at the conference had fascinated him. While some considered him one of America's experts in the future of drone technology, several of the proposals and concepts presented at the conference impressed him. Many were new to him, and he had made notes to follow-up on them after he returned to the States.

The small beach town wouldn't wake up for another hour, but he figured his boys would be up soon, wanting to go back to the beach. He started planning out the day's activities in his mind when a new, shiny deep blue Mercedes sedan pulled up to a stop next to him.

"Dr. Hockenberry," an attractive, dark-haired woman said in a heavily accented voice through the open passenger window.

"Yes," he replied, not recognizing her.

"Sorry to bother you, but did you leave this at the conference?" She held out what looked like a wallet.

"What? No, I don't think so?"

She spoke again, but she did so softly he couldn't make out what she said. He stepped closer to the car.

"Or this?" she asked, bringing out another small object from her lap.

Hockenberry never recognized the small dart pistol. The woman fired it, and the tranquilizer's effect was almost instantaneous. A large man emerged from the driver's side of the car, came around the car, and lifted Hockenberry up off the sidewalk. The man put him into the back seat of the Mercedes. Before getting back into the car, he picked up the bag of churros.

"Breakfast," he said to the woman.

The car drove away, leaving two churros on the sidewalk.

Chapter 2

Professor Hideki Jungson, picked up his pace as the trail took a downhill turn. He looked over at his running partner.

"What do you think the government's response will be, Sache?" he asked.

"They will be interested, but whether they will want our material but not us, or they will accept our offer will be the big question," Sache replied.

The two had been friends and coworkers at the Tokyo University for nearly a decade. They had collaborated in a variety of new patents and co-chaired a small research and development company. Their latest work resulted in a more effective way to make miniature solar cells more efficient. Scientists and manufacturers have continuously sought to decrease the size of solar cells while increasing output. Professor Jungson believed they had discovered the next big evolution in that effort.

The low clouds around Tokyo kept the temperatures cool but also trapped the humidity. Both men were sweating more than usual.

"I'd be less wet if it would start raining," Sache said.

Jungson nodded in agreement. He noticed two runners coming in their direction. Neither looked like they had dressed to be out jogging.

"Look at these two. The big guy looks funny," he said.

"Maybe they have an emergency."

He wondered if Sache might be right. The two instinctively slowed as they approached the man and woman running towards them.

"Are you okay?" Sache asked.

Rather than answer, the two veered and crashed into them.

"What?" Hideki asked, but before he could get another word out, the woman jabbed him with a small hypodermic needle. The world started swirling around him. The last thing he remembered, or thought he remembered, was the big man slicing open his friend's throat.

Chapter 3

"Mr. Smith, your phone is making a hell of a racket over there," the teenager pointed to Clint's gym bag across the room.

"Call me, Clint, Scott. I'm not that old," he said and walked over to his phone. He'd been coming to this new gym almost every day for the last month. Scott had the job to make sure everything was put back in its proper place after a customer left. Clint liked the kid's attitude and had asked him more than once to call him by his first name.

The phone indicated he missed a call and had received a text. He glanced at the text, "How's the new car? Call me. B"

Clint smiled. He needed a new car, but he didn't have one, and Buzz knew it. His current Lincoln sedan had been shot full of holes, and the quick patch job he had done left the car looking like it had a bad case of acne covered with a very thin coat of makeup.

He picked up his stuff and left the gym. Outside, he walked down the alley, crossed the road, and found a spot on the beach where no one was near him. He called Buzz.

"Hey, Clint, how's the weather down there?" Buzz asked.

"Hot, like it always is. What's up?" He didn't feel like small talk.

"We need to get you over to Madrid ASAP."

"Okay. Can you tell me what's going on?"

"I'll tell you in person in Madrid."

"She's letting you leave D.C.?"

"We've got good legitimate cover. Can you make the five-thirty flight out of Houston tomorrow?"

"To Madrid?"

"Yes."

"Shouldn't be a problem. Will I need anything special?"

"No, but plan on a week's worth of clothing," Buzz said. "I'm sending you the flight and hotel reservations now."

"Okay," Clint said and looked at his phone. The text hadn't arrived.

"By the way, I've gone to the trouble to get you a trade-in for your car. I'll explain in a different text. See you in Madrid."

"Wait a minute," Clint said but realized that Buzz had clicked off.

Buzz, his boss's deputy, had been his primary contact since he started working for Section years ago. Clint liked him, thought he was a fair and reliable man, but he didn't need Buzz to pick out a car for him. Unless, he thought, they gave him one of those James Bond cars with all the gadgets. The thought made him grin, but as they had never given him a car or offered any kind of a deal with a car, he wondered if Buzz had been kidding him.

The text came in a few minutes later and included flight and hotel reservations. The text also included instructions to park at an off-site parking lot near Houston International where a spot had already been reserved and prepaid. It didn't include anything about a new car.

Clint felt more than ready to get back to work. He had been idle for nearly two months. Theresa Deer, his boss, had told him he needed to keep a low profile for a while. Seemed like she was saying that a lot lately. Of course, his paycheck kept coming in, but his last outing had left a bad taste in his mouth. He was ready to move on.

After getting situated in his aisle seat, Clint thought the trip might be one of those rare smooth ones that make travel enjoyable. The drive from South Padre Island to Houston only took a few hours, and he located the parking lot without a problem. Even the security line at Houston International was surprisingly short. But then, the woman sat next to him.

She seemed pleasant enough, and they were in business class, so she wasn't crushed against him, but before they took off, she started coughing and repeatedly blowing her nose. She also wanted to talk to him. Clint wanted to read or sleep. For whatever reason, she thought Clint needed to know all about the divorce her daughter was going through.

By the time the flight attendant came around offering drinks, the woman already had a pile of used tissue on the small table she had positioned in front of her. The attendant raised an eyebrow at Clint who in turn shrugged his shoulders in a "don't ask me" manner.

The most recent outbreak of the newest coronavirus variant had been dying down, but Clint didn't like this lady, Melinda or Melissa, or whoever she said she was, coughing all over him. He didn't want to spend this trip in quarantine in some foreign country. He had applauded the decision to drop the mask mandate on planes, but at the moment, he wished he could double mask the woman. Maybe a tight plastic bag over her head, he thought and smiled.

About two hours into the flight, the attendant brought a mask to the woman. "Please, ma'am, put this on, a few people on the plane are concerned about your coughing."

"Oh, it's nothing," she said, accepted it and put on the mask.

"Thank you," the flight attendant said and walked away.

"Did you say something?"

"Not me," Clint said.

The woman stifled a cough under her mask and turned her head away from Clint. A few minutes later, Clint thought she may have fallen asleep. He mouthed a "Thank you" to the attendant the next time she walked by. She winked at him and gave his shoulder a slight pat.

The rest of the flight passed in relative silence. Clint took a short nap and finished reading his book just as the plane was touching down at Barajas International Airport in Madrid. He took a taxi to the Tres Noches Hotel and was pleased that his room was ready for him.

"This is for you, too," the old man behind the counter said, handing Clint a letter along with a room key.

The hotel was a small boutique hotel off the main streets but not far from the city center. Clint set his suitcase on the floor and sat down at the foot of the bed to read the letter.

"Please meet me at the Hungry Hunter at 7. It's close to the hotel -- B"

Not much of a note, Clint thought. Buzz rarely left D.C., and once told Clint that if it wasn't for him, he might have never gotten out of the city. The remark surprised him, as did a lot about Section, or Special Section, the ultra-secret government agency that employed him. Hidden under a couple layers of secrecy and subterfuge, only a couple people in the government knew about the agency.

The hotel had a very small dining room that doubled as a library. One older gentleman sat by the door reading a newspaper. Clint wondered when was the last time he saw someone reading a paper newspaper. He grabbed the only table near the window.

The lunch menu was set daily. You could take it or leave it. Today, it was bean soup, roast chicken, fried potatoes and wine. The menu did not offer a selection of wine, one could have the house wine or not. A young man dressed in black slacks and a white shirt approached him and asked if he wanted lunch.

"Yes, please," he responded in English before realizing he should have used the meager Spanish language skills he possessed.

One of the advantages of a set menu is that you don't have to wait long for your meal. Within minutes of ordering, the waiter returned with a tray, carrying a small glass carafe of red wine, a plate of food, and a small bowl of soup.

As Clint started to eat, he noticed the man with the newspaper stand up and start walking toward him. The man's eyes focused on the plate of food rather than on Clint.

"That looks good," he said with an English accent. "Yesterday they had the roast beef plate."

Clint swallowed. "Have you been here a while?"

"No, only the past three days. My daughter is attending the university here, and my wife and I are visiting her this week. They're out shopping at the moment. I thought I'd rather stay here and relax, but the bloody news has me all upset again. I do think the world is going mad."

"You'll get no arguments from me," Clint said.

"Some idiot purposely plows a car into a crowd killing and wounding people. One tribe in Africa wipes out an entire village, women and children included, belonging to a different tribe. What motivates these people?"

"I've no idea."

"Me neither. I'd join you for lunch, but I'm supposed to be waiting for my girls. Have a good day. Oh, you can have this," he said, dropping the English language newspaper onto the table before leaving the room.

Clint picked up the paper, the Financial Times, and glanced at it. The front-page headlines were full of doom and gloom articles. Inflation getting out of hand, another strange disease had found its way into Europe, allegations of government corruption, and so on. He flipped through the paper, not reading any of the articles in depth. He wondered if any of the articles might relate to why Deer had sent him here, but there was no way to know.

After eating his lunch, Clint went outside to try to walk off his jet lag. He'd been to Madrid before, but he was not familiar with the area around the hotel. With over three million inhabitants, he believed Madrid was the largest city in Spain. He had contemplated taking one of the thousands of self-guided walking tours now available online, but decided to pick a location as a goal and settled with the Prado Museum.

His phone indicated the walk would take approximately thirty minutes. The one-mile distance seemed perfect, but neither the phone nor his own calculations took the crowds on the sidewalks or the hot midday sun into consideration. Rather than make his jet lag disappear, it seemed to compound it. About two thirds of the way to the museum, Clint decided to turn around. His goal now was to take a nap.

Chapter 4

"You look like crap," Buzz said, as he approached Clint outside the restaurant.

"I don't know if it's simply a bad case of jet lag, or if the woman with the plague sitting next to me on the plane gave me something. I'll be fine, how about you?"

"Excellent. This is a great city. How's the hotel?"

"It's nice," Clint said, and they both entered the restaurant. The restaurant only had a few customers. Clint noticed that Buzz might have put a few pounds on since they last met.

"The dinner hour starts late here in Spain. I think we'd be considered early," Buzz said.

The small talk continued until after they ordered their meals.

"We've got something strange going on that has a lot of people worried," Buzz said.

"These days there are always a lot of strange things going on."

"True, but what has her interest piqued at the moment is the disappearance of four scientists."

Clint knew Buzz was referring to Theresa Deer. "Scientists?"

"Yes, and all related in some way to drones. First there was a Melody Spencer from Boston. She disappeared without a trace a little over a month ago. Then a Henry Dean vanishes a few days later. Ten days ago, Maurice Hockenberry was seen being kidnapped while on vacation in Spain. Finally, a couple days later, Hideki Jungson was taken while jogging near Tokyo University. In his case, his running partner was murdered."

"Who is taking them?"

"She's not ready to say yet. All the major intelligence agencies in the world have an interest in this. If any of the usual suspects are involved, we're not picking up any indicators. A few theories are being pushed that may have merit." Buzz took a sip of his wine and looked around the room.

"Which are?" Clint asked and coughed into his napkin.

"A third party being funded by one of the usual suspects, a criminal cartel, or a terrorist group looking to expand its arsenal. I like the third possibility, the terrorist group."

"What do they hope to gain?"

"It's puzzling, that's for sure. The four scientists are experts in their field, and while they all have different jobs currently focused at different objectives, combined they are capable of producing a very sophisticated drone. More worrisome, this could be a smaller, deadlier drone."

"Why the worst-case thinking?"

"Nothing else fits. Murder, kidnapping, the international aspects all make this look bad, really bad," Buzz said.

"No ransom notes?" Clint asked.

"No, nothing."

"What am I supposed to do?"

"The usual. Wait until we get some kind of fix on who's responsible. My guess is you won't have to do anything. Everybody has their net out. One of the agencies will locate them, and like usual, it will turn into an international goat-rope trying to get everything coordinated before they swoop in."

"Then why bring me here?"

"You know how she operates. The best intel we have is the trace of a plane that within a day of three of the disappearances flew into the region."

"The region?" Clint asked.

"Yes, the Mediterranean Sea. Each landed at a different location, but the three locations were all along the coast of the Med. We think the victims were offloaded to a boat and taken somewhere. However, we have no common boat to correspond with the landing sites."

"I thought you said four scientists have disappeared. Only three planes?"

"Hockenberry was on the coast of Spain when he disappeared. He likely went straight to a boat."

"Makes sense."

"We shared this theory with the Community, but no one has given it much credence."

"So, I wait?"

"Yes."

"How long will you be in town?"

"Three more days, maybe four if I can talk her into letting me stay an extra day."

Clint grinned, "Good luck. I don't understand why anyone rich enough and sophisticated enough to pull off the four kidnappings, couldn't simply buy whatever drones he wants. Why go through all this trouble?"

"Other than secrecy, I don't know why either. Any drone purchased would have a record or something else in its design, or whatever, that would give away its manufacturer, its distributor, and so on. If you make your own, there would be no trail, plus you can design it for any purpose you want."

"Still, it seems like a lot of effort."

"Yes, unless you have big plans," Buzz said.

"Assassinating a world leader?"

"Very possibly. Maybe assassinating a bunch of them. Attacking a nuclear power plant? Who knows? Create a sufficient number of tiny killer drones, and who knows where your limits are?"

"Could there be some other objective in grabbing all these people, scientists?"

"Could be, but the consensus is whoever is behind this is focused on making drones smaller and more lethal."

"I imagine there must be limits that we have already reached. Drones are no longer new technology," Clint said.

"That's right. Kind of makes the whole thing very hard to understand."

"Is there any evidence that such a drone has been used against a target of any sort recently?"

"No, I mean most governments and hundreds of companies possess drone capability. I'm sure they use them, but nothing has been reported in any intelligence channels indicating a rogue entity has used drones for some nefarious purpose."

"Nefarious?"

"Yep, likely describes your behavior when you're on a date."

Clint grinned. "Seems like I could be here a long time."

"Maybe. Worse places to be stuck."

"Do you think there might be more kidnappings?"

"No way to tell," Buzz said and glanced around the room.

"If the scientists were put on separate boats at different locations along the Mediterranean coast, have you had any luck in finding a common destination?"

"No, the CIA did spend a little time looking at our theory, but ultimately, I think it was something that they didn't want to dedicate the resources. Can't blame the experts at Langley, but I think they've become too reliant on technology."

"I guess it would be easy to transfer a person from boat to boat along the coast anyway, and it would be like that shell game."

"Yep, that too," Buzz said. He raised his glass of wine. "Cheers."

Chapter 5

Dr. Maurice Hockenberry fell to the floor after being shoved violently through the open doorway. He didn't know how many days it had been since they kidnapped him. They had kept him drugged while they transported him here, wherever here was. He finally came to his senses in a small, windowless bedroom, and had remained there without contact for at least one day. Someone did drop off his one meal. The person did not say a word to him. He came with an armed guard who stood silently in the background.

On what he believed was his second day here, the man who had brought him his meal brought him two matching white outfits to wear. Two pairs of pants and two shirts. They looked like what might be worn in a laboratory or perhaps a hospital. The man instructed him to put them on and to follow him.

Although the two guards who escorted him to this different room had said nothing, being brought to this room gave him some hope he might finally discover why he had been taken. They closed the door behind him. Within minutes, the door opened again and the guards tossed in another man.

He spoke something in a foreign language. Maurice thought he looked Asian.

"Are you okay?" he asked the man. He noticed this person wore the same white pants and shirt.

"Where are we?" the man replied in English.

"I don't know. A man and a woman kidnapped me, and I was brought here."

"That makes two of us. What's your name?"

"Maurice Hockenberry, and yours?" He sat in a chair and didn't make an effort to stand.

"Hideki Jungson. What are we doing here?"

"I don't know. One minute I was walking down a street in Spain and the---"

"Spain?"

"Yes, my family and I were vacationing in Spain."

"They kidnapped me near Tokyo," Hideki said.

"Why?"

"Seems like I asked you that a minute ago," and despite their situation the two grinned at each other. "I'm still woozy from the drugs they had me on."

"Do you know when you got here?"

"I think just yesterday."

"I've been here two or three days. I'm not sure. I don't remember arriving. They won't tell me anything," Maurice said.

The door opened, and another man, wearing the same white attire, was pushed into the room. He swore under his breath at the guards. The door shut.

"Who are you two?" he asked gruffly. His accent and red beard gave Maurice the idea he was from Scotland or Ireland.

"I'm Maurice Hockenberry."

"I'm Hideki Jungson."

"Damn, they are building an all-star team. I've already told them I'm not participating. No matter what they do to me or Melody. They can go to hell."

"What do they want us to do?" Hideki asked.

"Who's Melody?" Maurice asked.

The door opened, and a woman was pushed in.

"Meet Melody," the bearded man said.

The door closed, and Maurice heard the door being locked.

"What is going on?" Maurice asked.

"What happened to you?" Hideki asked.

Maurice followed his eyes to Melody's face and noticed it was bruised and swollen.

"They beat her," the bearded man said.

"Why? And who are they? Who are you two?" Maurice asked.

"Because they can. I'm Dr. Melody Spencer. They want us to build very small, very lethal drones."

"They want ones that can travel forever, see through anything, and kill or destroy anything. They're nuts, and I've told them that," the bearded man said.

Maurice recognized the name Melody Spencer. She was famous in the drone world, but he had never met her.

"Who are you?" Maurice asked the bearded man.

"I'm Dr. Henry Dean."

Another name he recognized.

"Why do they want us to do this?" Hideki asked.

"Come on, you tell me. They want to kill people and destroy things. They aren't with any government. They are obviously terrorists or part of some crime cartel. I'm not going to be part of any project that may kill innocent people," Dean said.

"Me neither," Hideki said.

"Good for you. They'll just have to go out and kidnap some other people," Dean said.

"It's not that easy," Melody said.

At that moment, the door opened and three men walked in.

Two were armed, and one appeared to be their leader. The two guards had what appeared to be the typical uniforms of a private security company. The other man had on dark slacks and a pullover dark blue sweater.

"Please, let's sit around the table," the leader said.

Maurice realized they were in a small conference room.

"No, not you Dr. Dean. You've been very outspoken how you don't wish to help us."

"Damn straight," Dean said.

"Why don't you sit there," he motioned with his hand to a hardback chair against a wall.

Dean did as he was told. The rest sat in the chairs around the table. Maurice noted they all were facing Dean.

"Are we all comfortable?" the leader asked.

No one answered him.

The leader nodded to a guard who held what Maurice thought was a sawed-off shotgun. The guard took one quick step towards Dean, raised his weapon, and shot Dean in the face.

Chapter 6

Clint sipped on his coffee and watched the people stroll around the Plaza Mayor, Madrid's large "town square."

"Back again this morning?" Steffi asked.

"You, too," Clint responded.

She took a seat next to him and sat her coffee cup on his small table.

"This is the perfect coffee shop to watch the whole plaza," she said.

"We don't have places like this back in the States."

"We do in Belgium. Must be a European thing," she smiled.

"I like it," Clint said and looked around at the large open courtyard.

"It's five hundred years old, I think. That's what someone told me."

Clint met Steffi two days earlier at this same outdoor café. They were each alone at separate, adjacent tables and had decided to join each other while they drank their coffee. Her parents owned an apartment in a nearby residential high rise.

"We used to come here each summer for a few weeks. Now, they think they're too old to travel much, but I still have fond memories, so I have started spending more time down here. My Spanish has gotten pretty good."

He was happy to see her again, and it wasn't because he had gotten bored sitting around waiting for something to happen.

"Five hundred years, that's older than the United States."

"Your country is like a baby when it comes to most

countries."

"Do they decorate the plaza for Christmas?"

"Yes, it's beautiful. You know, you made me think about my time down here after our last conversation. My job allows me to work from anywhere, so maybe I'll spend even more time here in Madrid."

"Good for you. Inventory control, right," Clint said, remembering their first conversation.

"Yes, but more so than what's in one store. We try to look at hundreds of stores, track their current inventory, and stay ahead of the flow in the supply lines. As you might guess right now, we are not having our finest hour."

"Not your company's fault though," Clint said.

"No, not at all. You didn't mention what you do, Clint?"

"In between jobs at the moment."

"But visiting Madrid, you must be part of that idle rich I keep hearing about."

"Not quite, but luckily, I do have a little saved up. I'm actually working on that next great American novel."

"Sounds interesting, have you finished it?"

"Ha, not hardly."

"Too bad you weren't around here when Hemingway was. He had a nice little group that hung around him. You could've joined in."

"I thought he was in Paris," Clint said.

"Yes, he was. Every year, though, he would spend a month or so in Spain, running with the bulls, going to bullfights, drinking brandy, and all that stuff."

"What a life."

Steffi's phone rang. She looked at it and stood up. "Hi

Michael, what's up?" She gave a slight wave at Clint and walked off.

Clint watched her walk away. An attractive woman, Clint thought, with her short blond hair, maybe too short, and pretty blue eyes. The light blue blouse she wore went well with her eyes. He guessed she was within a few years, either way, of his age. Forty wasn't that far away, and he couldn't believe it. He still felt like a young man. His phone buzzed in his pocket.

"How's Madrid?" Theresa Deer asked.

"I like it here. How are you doing?"

"Busy. I need you to leave for Innsbruck today. We'll keep your hotel room for you, at least through the week."

"Innsbruck? Sounds nice."

"I've put you on the express train. Better that way. Your tickets and hotel confirmation are being sent to you. Buzz will give you the details. I'm playing some hunches here, so it may be a waste of time, but if you've never been there, Innsbruck is a beautiful city."

"Sounds like fun."

"Just keep a low profile," she said and hung up.

Interesting call, he thought, and hoped Buzz did have a few answers for him. He left the café, looking around for Steffi as he did. He didn't see her.

Buzz waited for him in front of the hotel. "Can we go for a walk?"

"Sure, Deer said you could explain all this to me."

"I gave you the background the other night. What's happening now is more subjective. We have found a name mentioned twice in some intercepts that can theoretically be associated with past intercepts we believe are related to the prior kidnappings," Buzz said.

"Theoretically associated with message traffic that might be related to something else? What you might call a long shot?"

"Yes, very much so, but you know how she gets."

"What am I supposed to do? I'm not a collector," Clint said.

"I know, and she knows."

"Has she shared this with the rest of the Intelligence Community?"

"Of course, but to the best of our knowledge, no one is acting on it."

"What do you have?"

"A Kimberley Mose, there might be an accent in their somewhere. She's a PhD, a scientist working on the miniaturization of electrical circuits. Some of her past work has dealt with drones. Supposedly, she's tops in her field. Mix of French and Swiss, now working in Innsbruck. Her name has popped up twice."

"I would think the French, Swiss, or Austrian security people would be interested."

"Me, too, and they may be, but we haven't seen anything or gotten any feedback."

"I still don't understand what my role is in this. I'm not a body guard, either."

"This is a little different, I admit. However, your role will be the same. We still want the locals, the CIA, or some other allied service to swoop in and capture the bad guys. We'd rather stay out of it. As you know, though, the legitimate services are woefully inadequate in some areas."

"Going back to my role in all this," Clint said and raised his eyebrows.

"Go to Innsbruck and, as unobtrusively as possible, put an eyeball on Dr. Mose. We have to assume other people will be watching her, so be careful. We'll have more data to help you once you're there."

"Am I supposed to stop her from being grabbed?"

"At this point, no. The consensus is that they are being taken somewhere. They're not being killed, at least not right away."

"You hope to see where they go," Clint said.

"Yes, but we don't want you to follow them."

"This is making less sense than more, Buzz."

"Minor advantages, Clint, but they do make sense. Waiting there is no worse than waiting here. You may see something that could help. A license tag number, a face of one of the kidnappers, you'll see the target and be able to recognize her in case you run into her down the road."

"You know I didn't bring a weapon with me when I came."

"I know. No need to bring one on an international flight. We can easily get one to you wherever you are. Secrecy, as you know, is priority number one."

"Not my safety?" Clint grinned.

"A close number 2 or maybe 3, but we'll have a package for you in a locker at the train station in Innsbruck."

Chapter 7

"This can't be happening," Maurice broke the silence and said to his fellow two scientists.

They had sat in silent shock for at least a minute. Hideki had cupped his face with his hands.

"Believe it. These are nasty people," Melody said. Despite her blunt response, Maurice saw her eyes begin to water and her right hand start to shake.

"What do they want? They killed him and simply left the room." Hideki spoke in a hushed voice.

"It's like Dean said. They want us to build very small, very lethal drones," Melody said, blinking back any tears that may have wanted to escape her eyes.

"They're already being made for various militaries. Why don't they just go out and buy them?" Hideki asked.

"We talked about that a hundred times. It may not be as easy as you think. Plus, doing so would leave too many ways for them to be identified. They want to be able to use the damn things and leave no trail behind in case one gets intercepted."

"Who would they want to kill?" Maurice said, his mind finally getting focused on the discussion.

She shook her head.

"Why do they think we'll help them?" Hideki asked.

"You want to end up like him?" Maurice pointed toward Dean.

"They will threaten your families, too. Dean didn't have anyone. Now, they'll replace him. By the way, they are listening to us all the time," Melody said.

Both Hideki and Maurice looked around the room.

"How can you stay so calm?" Maurice asked. His fists clenched and the veins in his forehead swelled.

"Calm? I'm not calm, but I've been through this for a couple weeks now. The beatings, the abuse, the threats to my family. Maybe I'm becoming immune."

"What if we all say no?" Hideki asked. "They wouldn't kill us all."

"Not right away. They would first do something horrible to your wives or children. They might make you watch it online. Try to convince you that way."

"Oh, my God," Maurice said.

"These people are not like you and me. You need to get that into your heads."

"We need equipment, and they need a factory of some sort. They must take us somewhere. Maybe we can escape," Maurice said.

"They have it all here. Above us."

The two men instinctively looked up at the ceiling above them.

"Where are we?" Hideki asked.

"I've no idea."

"They must have employees that are not part of their scheme. Have you encountered any of the local people?" Maurice asked.

"We are kept segregated from any other employees they may have. I've had a few glimpses of them at work but have not had the opportunity to talk to any of them. We have our own office and about a handful of their own scientists, if you can call them that, who work with us. They deal directly with the factory workers, not us. I believe they are making the drones nearby."

"Who tells us what they want us to do?" Hideki asked.

"You'll meet him. He's got a solid but basic understanding of drones. You'll see. Seeing is much more effective than my telling you."

"You mean that guy in charge?" Hideki asked.

"No. This guy, the one who had Dean killed, is worse. I've never seen him express any emotion. He's cold and cruel. Pure evil this one," she lowered her voice with her last sentence.

Maurice once again glanced around looking for a microphone.

"I still can't believe this is happening," Hideki said.

"You will," Melody said.

"Once we help them make this thing, what then?" Maurice asked.

"Dean's belief was that they would use it to kill someone or destroy something. It's easier for me to think we might only be helping to destroy something."

"No, I meant what happens to us?"

"I try not to think that far ahead," Melody said.

"They will kill us. They killed my friend," Hideki said.

The door to the room opened, startling the three, and a guard pushed a cart into the room. On top of the cart sat a tray of food. Three hard rolls, three bowls of soup, and three glasses of water. The guard left.

"Prison food, for sure," Maurice said.

"Better than that." The man who had been there earlier and had ordered Dean be killed entered the room. The man glanced at the food. "The soup is quite good, and do not worry if we plan on killing you or not after your work is done here. So much of that depends on how you do here. You do not know who we are or where we are. What can you tell someone? Besides we could always kill you later if you did, or we could kill your entire family for that matter. Or worse."

"Please, why don't –"

"Quiet," the man interrupted Hideki. "Tomorrow, you start work." He turned and left the room.

A guard closed the door after him, leaving them alone.

"Someone must be looking for us," Hideki said.

"I'm sure someone is looking for us, but can they find us?" Melody said.

Maurice thought about that. He lived in the U.S., but they kidnapped him in Spain. How much time would either nation spend on finding him? He also thought about the man who had spoken to them. The man looked frail. He might have stood around five foot nine, but he was very thin and pasty looking with greasy black hair. Although he wasn't wearing glasses, Maurice saw depressions on the top of his nose where glasses might have sat for a long time. He did not appear to pose a physical threat, but Melody described him as evil. Maurice thought he, too, could sense the evil emanating from the man. Of course, the fact that he had Dean shot in the face a few minutes earlier may have encouraged that feeling.

"They have to give us access to computers and the internet. Can't we notify someone?" Hideki whispered this last sentence.

"We operate on a closed network. It's completely cut off from the outside world. They will get any piece of research or data you want, but they will do it from offsite somewhere."

"Think they will ever let us go? I mean can we believe what he said?" Maurice asked.

"Who knows? All we can do is hope," Melody said.

"How long have you been here?" Maurice thought she may have already told him, but at the moment, his mind didn't seem to be working right. He couldn't help but wonder what she had already gone through. The visible bruising to the left side of her face looked like it had been there a while. The coloring had already started to fade, but it still looked nasty.

"Two or three weeks, I don't think I've been here a month. I've lost track of the days. We have no access to clocks or calendars. I've been here long enough to learn to do what I'm told. It's a nightmare, so prepare yourselves. Do what you have to do to stay alive. It's like we're with the Borg on Star Trek, 'Resistance Is Futile'. All you can do is hope that one day you'll be out of this place. So how long have I been here? Long enough for my hair to get ratty." She reached up and grabbed a clump of her hair.

Maurice studied her while she was talking. He thought she was close to fifty years old, more than a decade older than himself. He knew she was intelligent, and despite the messy, black hair, he thought she was nice looking.

"I don't plan on dying here," Hideki said.

"Then do as they say," Melody said.

Chapter 8

Clint sat on a log on the side of a steep hill and snapped another picture of the large hawk circling above him. He had already taken photos of a variety of birds and a handful of squirrels. Enough, he thought, to show anyone who might question what he was doing only four hundred yards from the small villa owned by Kimberley Mose. The well-worn book on the birds in Austria he had purchased the day before would help, too.

His arrival coincided with Mose's week off from work. Fortunately, it didn't appear that she had any plans to go anywhere on a trip. Yesterday, he had watched the house for several hours in the morning from much further away. He had seen her jog the trail he was now nearby. She jogged with a man, but he hadn't been able to identify the man.

If they jogged and took the same trail today, they would pass a mere fifty yards from him but on the opposite side of a dry creek bed that dropped down some thirty feet between his vantage point and the trail. He imagined the creek bed would be full of running water each year during the spring thaw. The ample vegetation around him should keep him out of sight, yet he thought he would be able to get a good photo of them. He knew she might come alone today, but that was fine, too.

At the train station, upon his arrival, he had retrieved a small gym bag from one of the lockers. The bag contained a thousand Euros, a 9mm Beretta semi-automatic pistol, two clips of ammunition, a holster, and a light weight, black jacket.

Later, he secured the pistol along with its accessories in the spare wheel well in the trunk of his rental car. He didn't expect a need for it until he was assigned a target, and certainly didn't need to be carrying it if some local forest ranger or policeman became overly curious as to what he was doing out here.

From his vantage point, he couldn't see the house. He knew once they rounded the bend in the trail and came into view, he would only have a twenty to thirty second window to get his pictures. In the scant background Buzz provided him, he did say that Mose was an avid runner. Knowing that and seeing her run yesterday, Clint thought the odds were good that she would run again today.

He wondered if the man with her was a boyfriend, or if she had been provided with police protection, and the male runner was a bodyguard of some sort. Clint had learned that she had divorced her husband seven years ago after he was convicted of embezzling money from his employer. With not much more to do than wait, Clint let his imagination wonder if her marriage was already on the skids. Should a wife be loyal, forgiving, and stand by her husband while he spent a dozen years in jail for a white-collar crime?

Clint had never married and knew he might not be the best judge of spousal behavior, but he wondered if he was truly in love, would he divorce his wife if something similar occurred. Of course, this might have been one more to add to several earlier transgressions. The straw that broke the camel's back, as they say.

A movement in front of him, higher up on the opposite hill, caught his attention. It couldn't be Mose jogging, but there appeared to be two individuals, a man and a woman coming down the steep slope, approaching the trail.

Clint sensed trouble and brought his camera up to take a picture of the two. The man looked solidly built, while the woman looked slender. He had no sooner taken the picture when Mose and her jogging partner, the same one she had been with the day before, came around the bend. They did not seem to notice the two individuals above them. Clint took another picture.

He had to fight the desire to shout something to warn Mose. He didn't like the role he had been assigned. To do nothing seemed all wrong. Then he realized the two joggers might pass by before the other two got down to the trail. They did and were at least fifteen yards ahead of the other two by the time the two reached the trail.

Clint zoomed in, seeing through the camera's lens that both Mose and her running partner wore ear buds. He guessed they had no idea of the two racing to catch up to them from behind. About midway on the visible trail in front of him, the two caught up with Mose and her companion. The clumsy collisions left everyone falling to the ground. Mose got up first and raced off down the trail with her female chaser a few yards behind her. The two men rolled around on the trail until they fell over the edge and rolled down the slope.

The male assailant had what appeared to be a small knife in his hand and slashed at his victim whenever they came close enough to do so. His victim did his best to avoid the slashes and keep his distance, even while they both tumbled down the slope. At the bottom, the victim bolted upright and scrambled up Clint's side of the ravine. His assailant continued his pursuit. Both now raced toward Clint.

Clint could see a lot of blood on Mose's jogging partner's shirt, as he struggled to stay ahead of the bigger man. Suddenly, the man behind him leaped forward, swinging the knife wildly in front of him and catching his victim around the ankle with the blade. The jogger fell to the ground and almost started rolling back down the slope. The man with the knife stood, regripping the knife like he wanted to use it again.

"Hey!" Clint shouted and stepped away from the bushes. "Let him be."

The man stared at Clint and chose to ignore him, reaching down with his free hand to grab his intended victim. Clint moved closer to the two. His approach caused the attacker to let go and turn to face Clint. He said something in a foreign language that Clint didn't understand, but then he took two quick steps toward Clint, raising the blade and holding it out about a foot from his waist. This movement didn't need any translation.

Clint moved sideways a few steps, keeping the man a few yards away. It also made the man turn his back toward Mose's companion, who, Clint hoped, might get up and run away. He didn't, but he did watch what was going on.

The man grunted and lunged at Clint. He had little trouble avoiding the man's blade. Clint thought the man was winded from the chase. An advantage, but he knew better than to relax. The man closed the distance with three quick steps, and as Clint moved again to avoid him, the man dove at him. Dumb, Clint thought, but he supposed the man was counting on his own strength, along with the knife to do what he intended to do.

Clint blocked the man's knife hand and gripped the man's

wrist in an effort to twist it and force the man to drop the knife. A maneuver he had practiced and done many times, but never on the side of a steep hill. The man's free hand grabbed Clint's jacket. As Clint twisted the man's arm, the man rolled to his left to relieve the pressure, and in doing so, he pulled the two of them down the slope.

As they bounced off rocks and rolled over or through thick bushes, Clint kept trying to force the man to drop the knife. Somewhere before they came to rest at the bottom, the knife had fallen free. The man tried to scramble on top of Clint, but he was out of his league. In seconds, Clint maneuvered the man into position and broke his neck.

Clint carefully removed the man's wallet and took a picture of an identification card that had the man's photo on it. He took another photo of the man's face. Replacing the wallet, Clint stood and climbed up the slope. Mose's jogging partner, still on the ground, ended a phone call and didn't notice Clint until he was standing next to him.

"Can you stand?" Clint asked.

"I don't think I want to try. I called for the police and an ambulance. They should be here in ten minutes. Have you seen Kim?"

"Who is Kim?"

"She was jogging with me."

"No, but I'll go look for her. How badly are you hurt? Will you be okay here?"

"Yes. Is the man who attacked me gone?"

"Don't worry about him. He won't be coming back."

"I told them how to find me. Please go help Kim."

"I will," Clint said. He climbed down and then back up the

other side to the trail. He didn't need to be around when the police showed up. Deer would likely be angry at him for getting involved, but that couldn't be helped. The trouble had come to him.

Taking the trail in the direction that Kim ran would get him closer to where he parked and would get him there quicker than cutting through the forest. He ran for about four minutes before he reached the spot on the trail that he believed came closest to his car. He had not seen any sign of Kim or her pursuer. Kim was a runner and hopefully was able to run away from her attacker.

Clint had parked on the side of a dirt road that ran off the paved, two-lane road that would take him back into Innsbruck. The hike to the car took another five minutes. He started the car and drove off, hoping the police would not be taking this road. They would be suspicious of anyone driving near here for the next hour or so.

His phone buzzed.

"Take the next left. It's about a mile ahead of you. The Austrians have mounted a significant response to what they believe is a kidnapping attempt on Dr. Mose," Buzz said.

"I have some pictures to send to you."

"Are you okay?"

"Yes. Two people, a man and a woman attacked—"

"Please, just drive now. Deer said not to try to do anything else until you're safely out of the area."

Clint wanted to say he could talk and drive at the same time, but seeing his turnoff ahead of him, he remained silent.

"In a half mile you'll encounter a speed zone, so prepare to slow down. Shortly thereafter you'll be in an upscale suburb, and you'll find a shopping mall on your right. Park there and find someplace to kill an hour or so. We'll call you again in a half hour."

Shortly after ending the call, Clint saw two Austrian military helicopters race across the sky in the direction of Kim's villa. It had been less than fifteen minutes since the jogger had called the police. The Austrians were indeed not fooling around.

Clint found a restaurant in the mall and was enjoying an Austrian beer with sausage and sauerkraut when the call came.

"I received the pictures. We're working them. What happened?" Deer said.

Clint walked her through the morning's events, explaining how the trouble came right up to him, that he didn't go after it.

"My only concern is what Mose's jogging partner might tell the police," Clint said.

"He won't be telling anybody anything. He died before the rescue team got there."

"Damn, he didn't look that bad when I left him. I didn't check his wounds."

"Not your fault. They found the two men, but no sign of Mose."

"I didn't see another vehicle, and the woman chasing her didn't look strong enough to carry Mose far."

"I imagine they had a plan. The vehicle must have been close by. They wouldn't have wanted to carry her far. Not hearing anything may simply imply they were using an electric vehicle."

"Didn't think of that," Clint admitted.

"Any reason to think you might have left anything behind

that they can use to identify you?"

"No, I've considered everything. My only concern was the jogger providing the police with my description. Mose and the other woman chasing her never saw me."

"The Austrians are going all out on this. I can't blame them. The Swiss are fully cooperating. I think there are some business and family connections. Italy and France have voiced their concerns and support but haven't taken any serious steps yet. If she's not found before tomorrow, my guess is this will get worldwide attention."

"How many does this make?"

"You mean scientists?" Deer asked.

"Yes."

"Five. You would think they wouldn't need that many."

"Maybe they're fielding a basketball team. You know, scientists against the plumbers, something like that."

"I'll be sending you new instructions, but for the rest of the day play tourist," Deer said, ignoring his attempt at humor.

The call ended. Clint kept his phone in his hand and studied it for touristy things to do.

Chapter 9

Maurice settled into a routine. He knew he had no choice, and he wanted to stay alive. All three worked in a large room that looked more like a college laboratory than the office he had at work. Four days had passed since they shot Dean in front of him, but the vision remained with him. More than once it woke him up at night.

The work wasn't difficult, and he found himself liking both of his fellow prisoners. They had talked a lot about their personal backgrounds, excluding any discussion about their families. None wanted to share that information with their captors, who he believed were listening to their every word.

Melody had been there the longest and became their leader. She knew the four other men with whom they worked and was better at hiding any fear she might have with them. Their presence alone intimidated Maurice. He believed they had the same effect on Hideki.

"I told you this isn't easy. You wouldn't have kidnapped us if it was. Besides, every country in the world is trying to perfect this technology," Melody said to Jack.

Maurice knew that Jack wasn't his actual name. None of the four local scientists or technicians who monitored their activities on a daily basis had identified themselves. They shared nothing of their background. Jack was their leader, and the only one with whom they had any real communication. At Melody's suggestion, Jack had earlier agreed that was the name they could call him.

"Work harder and work faster. We need to have this done by the end of the month," Jack said.

"Or what? We don't get our bonuses?" Maurice said.

"You know what we will do. You should tell them, too," Jack said and left the room.

"What does he mean?" Maurice asked.

"Beatings. They will do nasty things to us to further motivate us."

"Will they kill us?" Hideki asked.

"I don't think so. Dean pushed them too far. He became too aggressive in his attitude toward them and way too vocal. But listen, the beatings are no fun either. We have to show them some progress, no matter how little," she whispered the four words.

"They have to know that we can only tweak the current levels of technology. They're crazy if they believe we can make some grand leap forward," Hideki said.

"I don't know what they believe. The other technicians, and that's what I think they are, not real scientists, aren't much help to us. Jack is the only one who regularly talks to us. We rarely see his boss, the man you met and who had Dean shot. You don't want to spend time with him."

Maurice thought he could see Melody shiver when she said that.

"He did that to you?" Maurice asked.

"He has his henchman to do most of the dirty work. He likes to watch and then join in at the end."

"There are a number of countries that would pay for this technology. Think one of them is behind this?" Hideki asked, changing the topic.

"Dean and I discussed this. You're right. We know it, and there are criminal cartels that would love to own some sophisticated drones, but that doesn't solve our current situation," Melody said.

"I know, but it is interesting to speculate and keeps my mind off thoughts of being beaten. Why are we working off schematics of the Hero drones used by the Israelis?" Hideki asked.

Melody looked at Maurice.

"He has a good point. I'd rather not dwell on what may happen to me either," Maurice said.

"We're using the Israeli technology because that is what they, Jack, told us to use. We didn't argue with them. Understand?" She looked at the two of them with eyes that willed them to think about it.

Maurice thought he did. The obvious being they didn't want to irritate their captors, but perhaps more important, why tell them there were more sophisticated drones already being made elsewhere.

"Understood," Maurice said.

"Me, too," Hideki said, but Maurice wondered if he did.

"Why did they beat you? You said you and Dean were able to make some improvements to the range and efficiency of the models."

"I think he just wanted to, Maurice. Maybe to show me they meant business, or maybe they wanted to have a little fun at my expense. Maybe they had already planned on killing Dean, and that's why they didn't beat him. I don't know."

"Jack said they need us to finish the job by the end of the month. Some of the things they are asking for are impossible.

They must know that," Hideki said.

"Enough talking, get back to work," Jack said as he entered the lab with another technician. "Focus this week on increasing the load the drone can carry."

"That will impact on the increased range you wanted before," Melody said.

"Don't let it," Jack said.

No one argued. Melody's warning had sunk in, and Maurice, for one, didn't want to get Jack agitated. He had no desire to see how much worse things could get.

"Okay, let's sit down and do a little brainstorming," Jack said.

The four of them sat down at a round table while the other technician busied himself with a computer at the other end of the room. Maurice tried to identify Jack's accent. He spoke fluent English, but something about the accent and Jack's olive complexion made Maurice think that it wasn't his native language. Maurice decided that Jack had Northern African or Middle Eastern blood in him, and that might explain the focus on an Israeli drone.

The brainstorming appeared to placate Jack, even though Maurice knew they hadn't accomplished anything. He hoped no one with an expert's knowledge had listened in on their session.

As Jack got up to leave, he said, "You'll get another member of your team tomorrow."

Chapter 10

Clint sat next to the window of the first-class cabin on the express train that would take him first to Paris and then on to Madrid. He drank coffee and slowly ate a hard roll he had smeared with butter, enjoying the view and the relative quiet. His mind kept bouncing back and forth between frustration and curiosity.

He knew his frustration would pass. It felt like the woman who had kidnapped Mose had bested him. She only had a minute's head start and had somehow disappeared with her victim despite his pursuit. It didn't seem logical that she could've subdued Mose and carried her off without any trace. He didn't see any paths connecting with the jogging trail which meant she would have had to carry or drag Mose through the dense forest and up one side or the other. He hadn't seen or heard a vehicle and only stopped his chase when he came to a straight stretch where the trail continued for several hundred yards. He should have been able to see them.

Of course, the obvious answer could be that Mose left the trail in an attempt to evade her pursuer and got caught off the trail. The dilemma of how a slender woman could carry another woman, at least as heavy as her, out of the forest to a waiting car could easily be solved if she didn't have to. At gun point, Mose may have simply walked.

The phone call from Buzz stoked his curiosity.

"They simply vanished. Everybody is asking what happened. Everyone is pointing fingers at each other."

"How about the boss's warning?"

"There's no blowback on that yet. She included it in an all-source threat assessment as a side note, suggesting it be further evaluated. The CIA and a couple European nations claimed they were looking into it, but it may not have received much priority anywhere other than Austria. Even there they were only doing the occasional residential drive-bys and heightened security where she worked."

"Who was the man?"

"Which one. Her running mate was a Juergen Schmidt, her personal assistant and maybe a little more. On his killer, we have no more than the ID data you shared with us, and that's likely fake. We'll get something, though. Only a matter of time."

"When you do, that should help," Clint said.

"And the photo of the woman is clear enough to let us do some digging. In the meantime, keep a low profile in Madrid."

"Hell of a way to run a railroad," Clint said.

"Don't feel bad. You gave us a big piece of the puzzle, and that's what this is, a giant jigsaw puzzle. Once we identify either the man or the woman, we'll be a lot closer to knowing what's going on."

"Any idea how long she'll want me in Madrid?"

"You know how Deer is. She gets these ideas. I believe she sent you to Madrid, so she could send you on to Innsbruck when she thought the time was right. We know the activity, whatever it is, is happening somewhere around the Med."

"Okay, I'll work on my tan."

"Do that," Buzz said and ended the call.

"What a way to run a railroad," Clint said aloud again to the empty room.

He had questioned his choice of occupation a dozen times since being recruited by Ms. Theresa Deer. She fascinated him as much as the small organization she ran. Created after nine-eleven, Deer led a team of hunters. That's what she called him, and how she described his role. She sent them after individuals who posed a very significant threat to the United States. He always operated alone, and other than a couple members of her staff, he had never met another person who worked for her. From the bits and pieces he had put together, he guessed she employed around ten others like him. Counting Deer, the number of people on her office staff only amounted to four or five.

She operated out of the basement of the US Marshal Service Headquarters with minimal oversight. Clint didn't know whom she might report to, but he knew it wasn't another government agency. Buzz had told him the small size of Section, or Special Section, he had heard both terms used, contributed to its secrecy. Buzz had said its entire annual budget was less than a half day's budget at CIA.

Clint didn't like having to "keep a low profile." It made him feel like he wasn't earning his pay, but both Deer and Buzz had told him repeatedly their preference was for the rest of the "good guys" to make the arrest or eliminate the target. It was only when the target eluded them, and it seemed like he or she would get away, that Clint would be given the green light. Even then, his presence and purpose were unknown to everyone else. No credit would be taken for the kill. No report would be written.

He didn't dwell on the morality of what he did. His time in the army had given him ample opportunity to do that. He may question the bigger policy decisions, and often did, but once he was engaged with the enemy, he did what was expected of him, and he did it to the best of his ability. Now, working for Deer, he also had the advantage of knowing his target had already been assessed by the entire U.S. and often the international intelligence community as a serious threat.

The train got him in late at night, but the streets of Madrid were still active. His phone buzzed when he reached his hotel.

"Glad you got back safely," Deer said.

"Pleasant train ride."

"Everyone's drawing a blank on Mose's whereabouts and the identity of her attackers. The type of knife found at the scene matches the blade type used to kill the professor in Tokyo. Japan has asked for everything the Austrians have. In the call your man in Austria made to the police, he did tell them that another man, you, had appeared out of nowhere and was fighting with his attacker. He gave no description of you. They are going with the theory that whoever took Mose also took you."

"Think she's still in Austria?"

"No. The Austrians do, because they believe they have all the ways out covered, but these guys are too good not to have an escape plan."

"I guess so. I'm curious how they got out of the woods in the first place," Clint said.

"Do you think the female who chased after Mose saw you?"

"Possibly. I didn't think so at first, but she could have been concealed in the forest and saw me as I ran by. Does it matter?"

"Not at the moment, but it might if you run across her in the future. I want you to stay there for the next few days, then I'll either bring you home or send you closer to our objective."

"Wherever that is."

"Exactly," Deer said.

Thinking about his situation didn't help, so he thought about his experiences with drones. In the military he had become familiar with them, especially the Switchblade drone. He thought they were probably still in use, but he believed a newer, improved drone, the Phoenix Ghost, had replaced it. More than likely, newer versions of that model were already being made.

An acquaintance of his had claimed in another thirty years drone swarms would replace all other weapon systems and fighting strategies. An interesting theory, but one for the science fiction guys, he thought.

Chapter 11

While the three scientists worked together all day, once the workday was over, they were each escorted back to their own rooms. They remained there, locked in, without any further contact with each other until the next day. Other than the odd noise coming from outside a room when something heavy was rolled by, the rooms remained silent.

Maurice found it difficult to keep up with the time and had long ago given up on guessing the day of the week. They routinely asked the others in the lab, but received conflicting answers or no answer at all. Even the computers they utilized had their date and time functions disabled. While he assumed they must work a long day shift, he had to admit they could be working at night as well as day.

The sound of someone crying, therefore, startled him. He walked around his room listening at the walls in an effort to determine from where the sound was coming. He found a spot across from his bed where he could put an ear against the wall and best hear her. A woman crying, he was certain.

"Melody! Melody is that you?" he shouted.

No answer, but the sobbing stopped. His door opened, and a guard peered in.

"Silence!"

"There is ..." Maurice stopped talking. Of course, the guard knew a woman was crying. He might make things worse if he kept asking questions. Besides, this guard had a very limited grasp of the English language.

A second guard came into the room. This one, the bigger of the two, had always made Maurice nervous. Something in his eyes didn't look right.

"You want her to hear you crying, or do you want for me to make her cry louder so you can hear her better?" the second guard said.

Maurice shook his head. "Please don't hurt her," he said, and suddenly felt like a useless coward.

The two guards left without saying another word.

Maurice sat down on his bed, wiping at the tears that had started to form. He didn't think he could feel much smaller. He slept little before they awakened him for the next day's shift.

"Melody, are you okay?" he asked after being escorted to the lab. She sat on a stool, studying her computer screen and looking the same as the day before.

"What do you mean?"

"I thought I heard you crying last night."

"Not me."

"It was a woman, I'm sure."

Hideki entered the lab.

"Hideki, did you hear a woman crying last night?" Maurice asked.

Hideki's eyes went to Melody.

She shook her head. "Not me."

"No, I didn't."

"Dean's replacement," Melody suggested.

Maurice nodded. It made sense.

They worked throughout the day, but no one new showed up. Through brief and almost silent dialogue the three agreed to a modification to increase payload capability. The modification was a no-brainer. A few countries had already integrated the modification into their systems.

Maurice wondered if the task was some sort of test. Any expert in the field of drones should have some basic knowledge of the improvement. On the other hand, he had come to think, like Melody, that Jack and the others were not experts. Either way, they all believed that the modification was something they could do without feeling too guilty about helping out their captors.

"This is good, really good," Jack said when they briefed him on the recommendation and had suggested what fixes he needed to make.

After the two guards locked Maurice in his room, he tried to get a better handle on his mixed emotions. He felt somewhat upbeat in the team giving Jack something that he appreciated and what Maurice knew was something that was already available in the right markets. However, he also felt guilt and shame for feeling upbeat at all. He wanted to tell Jack and all his captors to go to hell. He shouldn't be helping them, but he also wanted to see his family again.

He didn't hear another sound that night until a few minutes before the guards came to ensure he was up and ready for another day. He lay awake in his bed, waiting for the pounding on his door, when he was startled by a nearby shriek of someone in pain. He sat up and listened, but no other sound reached him. As before, he thought the sound came from a woman.

They escorted Maurice to the same conference room where they had killed Dean. Hideki paced around the room and barely looked up when Maurice entered.

"What are we doing back here?" he asked.

"I don't know," Maurice said.

"I've been here at least ten minutes. They've painted over the blood on the wall and cleaned the chair, but they left a piece of him on the floor." Hideki's eyes flashed down at a spot on the floor near the chair.

Maurice looked down and saw something. He turned his head away. He wasn't going to look at it.

"Come over here. We can turn the chairs and look at the door or something else. Don't look at it," Maurice said.

Hideki sat down in a chair next to him. "What are we doing here?"

"I don't know. I heard that woman again."

"What woman?"

"The one I heard crying," Maurice said.

The door opened and Melody entered. She glanced at them and looked around. Maurice thought he could see her shudder.

"Are you okay?" Maurice asked.

"Yes, but I don't like being back here."

Melody was still standing by the door when it was flung open, and a guard shoved a woman into the room with such force she collided with Melody. Both almost fell down.

The new person staggered away from Melody. She, too, was dressed in the all-white attire Maurice and the other two wore. She looked at the three scientists. When she looked back at Melody, she paused, and her eyes seemed to focus.

"Dr. Spencer, right? What are we doing here?"

"Good God, Kim? Is that you?" Melody said.

Kim nodded.

"Who are you?" Hideki asked.

"Hold on," Melody said. "Kim, are you hurt?"

"Nothing serious, but I'm being held prisoner here. They kidnapped me."

"We are all prisoners here," Melody motioned with her left hand toward Maurice and Hideki. "This is Maurice Hockenberry and Hideki Jungson. We're all scientists with a special interest in drones."

"What? I don't understand."

"You will," Melody said. "Gentlemen, this is Kim Mose. We were on the same panel at a conference five or six years ago."

"Dean's replacement," Maurice said.

"It appears so," Melody said.

"Henry Dean?" Kim asked.

The door opened and three armed guards entered followed by the same man that ordered Dean's death. Panic started to overwhelm Maurice, and he had to step back and put a hand on the table for support. He noted Hideki's face turn ashen white. Two of the guards had pistols holstered on their belts. The third guard carried the sawed-down shotgun.

"Sit down, please," the leader said in a soft voice that did little to hide the menace in it.

The four moved to the table and started to sit down.

"No, no, not you Hideki. Please, over here," he motioned to the chair against the wall where Dean had been sitting when they shot him.

"Agh," Hideki tried to speak. "No, no I want to sit here."

Two of the armed guards grabbed Hideki and forced him into the chair. The other three scientists could only watch. Maurice wanted to do something but felt frozen in time and place.

"Please," Hideki said and tears began to run down his face.

The leader grunted something to the third guard. The guard moved in front of Hideki and aimed the shotgun at his head.

Maurice couldn't breathe.

Suddenly, the guard lowered the shotgun and stepped back.

The leader smiled at them. "This is your last warning. Teach her quickly." He then focused his eyes on Melody. "She should not want me to come visit her. If I have to, I will come visit you again, too."

They left the room, leaving the four scientists alone. Maurice saw Hideki leaning over in his chair, his head in his hands. Melody held Kim's hands in hers. Kim appeared terrified, but Melody had the look of a marathon runner, bone tired but determined to keep running to the finish.

Maurice wanted to be more like her, to will himself to push fear aside, but he knew it would take every bit of will power he had, if not more. He was terrified. His hands shook, and he didn't know if he could speak.

Chapter 12

Clint studied the people as they moved through the large plaza. He had made this outdoor café his go-to spot for coffee and a light breakfast. This was his fifth morning since returning from Innsbruck, and he had settled into a daily routine. Awake at seven, he would walk a half mile to a large city park where he could run for thirty minutes. Dozens of people ran each morning in the park, several with their pet dogs. A handful ran everyday like him, and he had even reached the point where he nodded a hello to a few.

After the run, he would return to his hotel and do enough push-ups and sit-ups to feel good about it. He no longer counted. Then he would shower and walk to the café, staying on the shady side of the streets. The café's location in the plaza provided morning shade for its outdoor seating. In summer, in Madrid, the shade is always in high demand.

He played tourist in the afternoon, visiting museums, old churches, and even spent one afternoon at the zoo. In the evenings, he followed a travel magazine's recommendations for the best dining in Madrid. Keeping a low profile had been okay so far, but he knew he was becoming antsy to go operational or go home.

He took his time sipping his coffee. This morning he had ordered a croissant to go along with it. Yesterday, it had been churros. He had lingered a little longer at the café the last couple of days hoping that Steffi might show up. She hadn't, and he was about to leave when he saw her walking toward him from across the courtyard.

"Hello, Clint. May I join you?"

"Of course."

She looked at the crumbs on his plate. "Are you about to leave?"

"No, I need another coffee."

"Good." Steffi walked over to a woman cleaning a nearby table, said something and then pointed at Cliff. The woman nodded and went inside.

Steffi, dressed in white capris and a soft pink blouse, sat in the chair opposite Clint. She smiled but didn't say anything right away.

"It's nice seeing you again," Clint said.

"That day we were here together, and I received that phone call, well, I had to go back to work."

"To Belgium?"

"Yes. My boss had a car accident. He had to spend the night in the hospital, and at the time they didn't know how long he would be away from work. It ended up not being too long. So now, I get to add a week to my stay here."

"Everything okay?"

"Yes. How about you? Will you be here for a while still?"

"At least a few more days," Clint said.

"I wish I had the freedom to move about as I pleased."

"It gets boring. Any chance I can talk you into taking me to a good restaurant tonight? My treat."

Steffi smiled. "I could arrange something. Where are you staying?"

Clint mentioned the hotel, but Steffi didn't recognize it. She mentioned a restaurant unfamiliar to him, but he agreed to it.

"I didn't bring any fancy clothes," Clint said.

"People are casual here now. It's not like when I was growing up."

"That's good. I'd hate to embarrass you."

Steffi laughed. "So, meet at the restaurant at eight?"

"Will we need reservations?"

"I will take care of that," she said.

"I can come by and pick you up."

"No, no need. There's no place to park."

Clint guessed she wasn't ready to show him where she lived. That didn't bother him. Eating dinner with another person for once would be nice enough. The fact that this other person happened to be beautiful didn't hurt.

"I hope going out with me won't cause you any difficulties," Clint said.

"Are you asking if I'm married or have another man in my life right now?"

"I guess so."

"Then don't worry, there won't be some jealous lover showing up. How about you?"

"I've led a nomadic life the last few years. Never been anywhere long enough to establish any roots." He did wonder if her answer really answered the question.

"To two nomads," Steffi said and raised her coffee cup for a toast. After another twenty minutes of casual conversation, Steffi said she had to run.

"I'll be there tonight," Clint said.

"Me, too," she said and walked away.

Clint started to stand when his phone buzzed. He sat back down.

"Something happened in Nairobi," Buzz said.

"And?"

"Sorry, Dolly was saying something to me. A senior general was killed by what we believe was a drone attack. He was walking into a government building early this morning when he keeled over. At first, the few witnesses there thought it was a heart attack, but a small, nasty wound was discovered on the back of his neck. With all the street noise, nobody heard anything, but later they found a witness who said he thought he saw a large bee flying away."

"A drone?"

"That's the consensus thinking. The wound is not from any firearm we are aware of. His security contingent said no one approached him. We don't know much yet, and we haven't any idea why this general was targeted."

"What do you want me to do?"

"Nothing right now, but she did want you to know what happened. If we get something more, we may have to send you out with little notice."

"So, what do you think? A small, silent drone sneaks up and fires what, a smaller dart? Then it just flies away? With a drone that small, wouldn't the operator have to be close by?"

"I'm not sure, but smarter people than me are analyzing this right now. With these scientists being kidnapped, and now a likely drone attack on a general, the intelligence community is buzzing with theories."

"Why this general?" Clint asked.

"He was a rising star in his country, but other than that we don't know. CIA and State will likely come up with some good explanation. What most everyone believes, though, if this is related to the missing scientists, no one would go through all that trouble just to go after this one general."

"So, maybe a practice round?"

"Yes, but one that was on someone's list. Whoever is doing this must have had a reason or maybe a contract to go after him."

"Seems like we've seen this before," Clint said.

"And the interesting thing is last time it was all tied back to the Mediterranean area, too. Might be a coincidence, or it could be that's where the contracts are made."

"Well, you do have an interesting bunch of countries that touch the Med."

"Yes, you do," Buzz said.

"Is she keeping me here for a while longer?"

"Your guess is as good as mine. Everyone is still pulling up blanks on where Dr. Mose was taken."

"No flight data."

"No, but from Innsbruck you can drive to a number of port cities in less than a day. Sort of like the guy they grabbed in Spain. Too close to the Med to need to be flown anywhere."

"How does one set up a business to assassinate people? I guess the question is more how do you advertise without the whole world learning about you?"

"It can't work like that. We think it's more like someone wants to kill off certain key figures and then goes about creating his or her, I guess, own team of killers," Buzz said.

"It would be easier to hire a group of mercenaries and put them on salary or retainer."

"And, in this case, use technology rather than a group of human assassins. Of course, they had to employ the two that you encountered to go out and grab the scientists. Japan now believes they have identified the two entering Japan, but not leaving."

"Obviously they did," Clint said.

"Yes, and they entered Japan with false documents. Hardly surprising."

"Any other scientists coming up on Deer's radar?"

"No."

"That may be a good thing. I doubt if they will let any of them live when they are done with them."

"We feel the same way."

"By the way, why are you up so early?"

"This Nairobi thing. Deer will want a synopsis when she gets in."

"If I have a choice, I'd rather not go there."

"Yours is not to question why. Yours is but to do and die. Something like that, right?" Buzz chuckled.

Chapter 13

"This was one of Hemingway's favorite restaurants," Steffi said as they entered the old restaurant.

"Really?" Clint said, arching his eyebrows.

"Yes, I thought you would enjoy it. Maybe it will give you some inspiration for your novel. Even if it doesn't, the food is still good."

"This is great, thank you."

Restaurant Sorbrino de Botin was not very large and most tables already had customers. The server seated them near the door to the kitchen. The smell that drifted out to them every time the door swung open reminded Clint of the large, open pit barbeques that he had been to a few times in Texas.

"Smells good. Makes me hungry," Steffi said.

"Me, too."

"Can't believe I've only been to this place once before."

Their server came and they ordered the night's specialty along with a bottle of red wine.

"Do you have a large family, Clint?" Steffi asked after their order had been taken.

"No, only me, never had any brothers or sisters. How about you?"

"Oh my, yes. Three brothers and two sisters, and four cousins that were just as close. They have scattered all over the world now. Only my baby brother, Hans, has stayed nearby. Eryn, my older sister, lives in Denver. Married a Yank," she said with a grin.

"And not disowned?" Clint asked.

"No, no way, we're all happy for her. I've even traveled to Denver to visit her. I love the Rocky Mountains. Now, my cousin Neal married a Japanese woman. I think that was a little harder for my uncle to swallow. Such a difference in cultures and language, but he loves her now. The fact that she works in Luxemburg and makes a lot of money helps, too."

"That's normal behavior," Clint said.

"I know, but we also thought it was a bit ironic."

"We?"

"Most of us thought he was being prejudice, until he discovered how much her salary was and that she could speak English. Those things shouldn't matter."

"True, but to a parent, I think they usually do. I doubt if he wanted his son to move to Japan. It's so far away," Clint said.

"I hope that was all it was to it, but most European men see an Asian woman and automatically think they're working at the Thai massage parlor on the corner. There's too much stupid stereotyping. Sorry, but it's a sore point with me. Many are victims of human trafficking."

She was getting a little wound up, so Clint nodded but didn't respond.

"Sorry, that's not the best topic for tonight," she said. "Have you been to Japan?"

"Just passing through a few days, and, not to brag, I've been to a number of Asian countries. They are a bit of a culture shock. Not as much as the Middle East, but anywhere you go where the signs don't use our alphabet is strange and hard to get used to."

"I can imagine. So, tell me what is this novel you're writing about?"

"You mean the one I'm currently trying to write. I have a bad habit of giving up on one and starting another."

"That's a sure way to never finish but yes, the current one," Steffi said.

"It's sort of a psychological thriller. Two very competitive sisters are fishing with their father on a river in Alaska when their father has a heart attack. They are a couple days boat ride back to the main fishing camp. They see smoke from a chimney coming from a cabin in the distance. The two run to it for help and find a young man living there alone. The father dies, and they all get stuck in the cabin as an early winter storm strikes the area."

"Sounds interesting."

"And familiar, unfortunately, there are a handful of similar stories out there already. The plot in mine though is to build tension with the reader slowly coming to the realization that one of these three is going to kill one of the other two. But who is going to kill whom?" Clint said raising his eyebrows and grinning at Steffi.

"I think it could work."

"Maybe," Clint said.

"Might be too scary for me to read."

"It's too scary for me to write."

Steffi laughed, "Certainly you do some type of real work."

"I served in the military for a while. Since then, I have done a few things. Mostly, now I manage a few properties that I have and travel."

She looked at him like she was trying to see into his mind. He figured she correctly imagined there was more to him than he let on. Their dinner came, and their conversation drifted to their food and things to do in Spain. Clint paid for their dinner over Steffi's protests that it should be her treat.

"There's a taxi stand right out front," she said as they were walking out. "Will I be seeing you at the café tomorrow or later this week?"

"I hope so, but I'll be glad to share a cab with you?"

"Next time," she said, giving him a quick kiss on the cheek before walking away.

Clint watched her get into the cab. She smiled at him, waving with two fingers as the cab drove off.

"Interesting," he said out loud to himself.

The Madrid streets were busy with the normal late evening diners and revelers. After checking his phone to determine the distance to the hotel, Clint decided to walk instead of taking a cab. He imagined one could Uber here, too, but he wanted to walk off his dinner. He wondered if his walk would take him through parts of Madrid that the local police might suggest staying out of after dark, but decided the streets still had enough pedestrians to keep those who preyed on the solitary walkers at bay for another hour or two. He reached the hotel without incident.

The next morning, he didn't see Steffi at the café. He half expected her not to be there. She seemed to have a nice time at the restaurant, but her departure had him wondering if she had a bad experience in the past, or, like the song says, "she wasn't into you".

Buzz called him shortly after he returned to his hotel. "We need you to leave for Trieste, this evening. Can you handle that?"

Clint knew it was a rhetorical question. "Trieste? That's Italy, right?"

"Yes, barely. It's a large port city in the northeast corner of the country. It's got a lot of history and, for the most part, considered a safe city. But it does have some sections around the port that can be quite rough."

"Like Marseilles?"

"No. Marseilles is like Trieste on steroids. There is no comparison."

"Sounds like my kind of place."

"Don't bet on it," Buzz said.

"Why there?"

"She'll tell you. Same process as Innsbruck. We'll keep the hotel room in Madrid reserved for you. Flight and hotel reservations have already been made. We don't think you'll be there for more than a few days."

"I'll start packing," Clint said.

The two-hour flight to Rome got Clint in a quarter after seven. With only a forty-five minute layover, Clint decided to forego dinner at the airport. He hoped they served dinner late in Trieste, like they did in Spain.

Deer called while he waited. "You'll love Trieste. It's an old city with lots of sights."

"That's what I hear."

"This is a longshot, Clint, and I haven't shared it yet. Skipping the details, I think it's a possibility that Mose was taken to Trieste before leaving on a ship."

"Any target in Trieste?"

"No, but there is a slight possibility Mose could still be there."

"A rescue mission?"

"No, not at all. If we determine she's there, the locals can do that. Trieste is a stone's throw from Slovenia and Croatia. It may also be close to where the scientists are being kept. I want you to get familiar with the city. The better you know it, the safer you'll be if things get hot near there."

"Think it will?"

"No, not really, but I keep getting a nagging feeling we're getting closer."

"Anything new on the assassination in Nairobi?"

"No. The locals are holding everything close. I believe they are trying to build a case against an opposition party. There may be more bloodshed."

"Does the opposition have the capability to start killing people with drones?"

"Drones are common, but the size of this one and the way it killed seems to put it out of their depth. More likely a contract killing, which again goes back to our missing group of scientists," Deer said.

"Automating the killer for hire concepts. The nerds are slowly taking over. Pretty soon you won't need any hunters. You might only need a handful of drones."

"Don't think I haven't considered it. Buzz would be in heaven."

Clint grinned for a second, until he realized it wasn't really a funny thought.

"You remember when they killed that Greek millionaire in Las Vegas, drones were used. They were a lot bigger though," Clint said.

"Of course, I remember it. That's what made me focus on

the Mediterranean region in the first place. We took out the killer and the banker in that one, but maybe not the brains behind it."

Clint almost countered with the fact that the banker, as she referred to him, had been killed by those he had tried to kill, not by any hunter, but he knew she didn't need to be corrected.

"We'll stay in touch," Deer said and ended the call. His mind went back to that earlier mission Deer had sent him on involving the murders of a handful of the world's richest people. He had met the daughter of a Greek billionaire during that mission. As far as he knew, she still lived in Athens. Maybe at the end of all this, he would swing by to see her.

Chapter 14

Trieste at night appeared to be an interesting place. The cab ride from the airport to the hotel took him right into the heart of the city. Like Madrid, people were still on the streets and at the outdoor cafes, showing no signs of going home, despite it being nine o'clock. Clint grabbed a light dinner at the hotel's café. He could get acquainted with the city tomorrow.

The hotel's staff set him up with a bus tour of the city in the morning. Although Section's recommendation for him to get familiar with the city may have been more to keep him busy than trying to give him some tactical advantage, Clint knew such knowledge could indeed come in handy.

His bus tour group had finished a walk-through of the Museo Sartorio, and the bus started driving through a section of the city that appeared to be full of small shops and apartments when he saw her. He sat in a window seat. The bus had stopped for a red light. The light had turned green when he sensed someone staring at him. A dozen or so people were tangled together at a street corner waiting to cross. He looked at the group and saw her, or who he thought was her. The woman who had chased after Mose. The now dead man's accomplice in the kidnapping. He looked straight at her. She didn't avert her eyes, continuing to stare back at him.

The bus sped up and away. Clint considered shouting at the driver to let him off, but when he turned his head back to look for her one more time, he couldn't see the crowd at the corner, and the bus continued accelerating. As doubts entered his mind on whether the woman could be the one, he checked the pictures on his phone. One of them had a good shot of the woman's face, and yes, she was the one.

Initially, Clint thought he would get off at the next stop and find his way back to the intersection where he saw her. The bus didn't stop for another five minutes. By then, Clint realized he would have more luck going back to the intersection the next day around the time he saw her and watch for her. Besides, he knew he needed to brief Deer on the woman's presence. She may insist he stay away from her.

The bus stopped at another museum, the Museo Sveviano, and everyone got off. Clint followed the group into the museum, but after ten minutes he broke away from the tour. He walked down a dusty hallway that looked like it had been ignored for years and found a door to a room labeled storage. He opened it and went in. The fair-sized room had one window that supplied the room with its only light. Tarps covered everything in the room, and a fine film of dust covered the tarps. Dust floated through the beam of light coming through the window.

Clint started tapping out a text on his phone when the door behind him opened. He turned thinking for some inane excuse he had for being in the room. In the corner of his eye, he caught a flash of movement as a woman hurled herself at him. The blade in her hand reflected a ray of light and sparkled in the dimly lit room.

He leaned away from her, but she was fast, swinging the blade with her righthand at his throat, cutting his shirt collar and causing a button to fly off. As the knife blade continued on, it sliced across the knuckles on his right hand, causing him to drop his phone. Clint took a step back, recognizing the woman as the one he saw on the corner. The woman who had kidnapped Mose.

She continued her attack with a kick aimed at Clint's groin. His years of practice allowed him to instinctively deflect the kick. She followed the kick attempt with a slash of her knife aimed at his upper thigh area. Going after an artery, Clint thought, and he scooted back another step, running into a tarp-covered table or counter.

She attacked him again. Her left hand streaked at his eyes, followed immediately with a strike to Clint's belly with the knife. He slapped away the hand and fingers going for his eyes and lucked out when the blade got hung up in his belt buckle. He grabbed her knife hand milliseconds after the blade made contact, but if it wasn't for his belt delaying the knife's penetration, the blade would have cut three or four inches into him before he could have stopped it.

With a firm grip of her right wrist, Clint twisted her arm and spun her into the tarp. As she collided with the furniture, he stretched out her arm and drove the palm of his left hand through her elbow. He heard a snap followed by a loud gasp. The woman became limp for a second, and he thought she might fall down. Clint grabbed the knife out of her hand and started to step away.

As he did, the woman spun around and brought up a small pistol in her left hand. Clint knocked it away from her. She responded by leaping onto him and biting him on his shoulder. She tried to maneuver her head around to bite his neck. If her right arm was working, she might have been able to do it, but she had no leverage.

Still, Clint knew he had to do something quick. He spun her around again to get momentum and threw her away from him. She crashed head first into another tarp covered piece of furniture across the room. Clint hurried to her. She had somehow managed to reach her hand to the pistol. He leaned over to remove the weapon but noticed the odd bend to her neck and head. Using his handkerchief, Clint pulled the pistol away from her before rolling her over. She was dead. Her hand must have fallen toward the pistol.

Clint took a picture of her and searched her for any identification documents. She had nothing but a small wad of Euro notes. He moved her to a spot behind a tarp covered table or desk where someone coming into the room wouldn't see her. Clint pocketed her knife, as it had his blood on it, but left the pistol with her. He didn't see any blood on her hands or clothing. Looking around the room, he retrieved the button that she had sliced off his shirt from the floor.

Walking out of the room, he saw the tour group starting to line up to leave the museum. He wrapped his handkerchief around his hand to capture the blood oozing out from the shallow slice and put his hand with the handkerchief into his pants pocket. He joined an older couple talking about the morning's excursion.

Before Clint climbed into the bus, he noticed a solitary cab sitting off to the side of the road. The cab driver sat on the hood of his car watching the entrance of the museum. She must have followed the bus in the cab after she saw him. Like minds, he thought.

Chapter 15

"Received the photo. No ID?"

"No," Clint replied by text to Buzz.

He suspected they were not pleased with his confrontation. Killing people usually did not fall in the "keep a low profile" set of guidelines. They would most likely yank him out of Trieste as soon as flight arrangements could be made.

Clint had waited until after the bus had dropped everyone off at the end of the tour to send the text. The reply had come back almost instantly. He expected it would take Buzz and Deer a few minutes to consider a response. They would know that Clint had killed her. How else would he have been able to take the picture? Besides, sending in a photo after a kill followed Section's protocol.

The call came within seconds, not minutes.

"What happened?" Buzz asked.

"I saw her on a street corner while I was on the tour bus. She saw me. The bus drove off, so I didn't have a chance to confront her. I figured I'd tell you she was in Trieste and go look for her if you wanted me to. At the next stop, I found a quiet room away from the group to call you. That's when she came out of nowhere and attacked me. She was good, too, a professional."

"Means she must have seen you in Austria."

"She and Mose could have been off in the trees when I ran by looking for them."

"You okay?"

"Yes. In our struggle, I threw her away from me, and she hit her head."

"No witnesses?"

"No." Clint went on to explain where the incident took place, where he hid her, and what had happened from the time he left the room through the end of the tour. He mentioned the taxi.

"For her to follow you like that would imply to me that the man you killed near Innsbruck must have meant a lot to her."

"I thought so, too. She definitely wanted to kill me."

"No conversation?"

"Not at all, she was a pro."

"We still haven't been able to identify her," Buzz said.

"I imagine the locals might once she's been discovered. She may be from here or have family here."

"I don't think we want to rush her discovery," Buzz said. "I imagine Deer will want us to do a few things first anyway. Did you happen to see if the museum had any security cameras?"

"I didn't see any inside."

"Right now, there's no police chatter over there about finding a dead woman, so it doesn't appear the taxi cab driver searched and found her."

"He probably thinks she left without him, maybe skipped without paying her tab," Clint said.

"Yes, but when he hears of a woman found dead in the museum, it's possible he'll come forward."

"The place had a lot of visitors today. Another bus group was going in as we were filing out. It's one of their top tourist attractions. If she isn't found in the next forty-eight hours, it may be impossible for the police to narrow down their search for a suspect."

"That's why we're checking on any security cameras in the area."

"Do you want me to hang around in Trieste much longer?"

"The boss will let you know later today. In the meanwhile, try not to kill anyone else," Buzz said and ended the call.

Clint had done enough playing tourist for one day, so he found a nearby restaurant and ordered a late lunch with a large beer. After his beer arrived along with a plate with a hard bread roll on it, but before his lunch came, Clint found the restroom to do a close inspection of his hand. The handkerchief had contained the blood flow. He washed his hands doing his best to clean the long slice without causing more bleeding. Once he had blotted the wound with the paper towels, he thought he could return to the table with the bloody handkerchief safely concealed in his pants pocket. He took an extra paper towel with him in case he needed to blot away any blood that might continue to ooze from the wound.

It did, and when the waitress came with his lunch she noticed right away. "Oh, you've cut yourself," she said in very accented English. They had already ascertained when Clint ordered that her English was better than his Italian.

"Yes, I sliced it this morning when I was working on my car. A sharp piece of metal."

"Do you want a band aid?"

"No, I'll be fine. I grabbed a piece of paper towel," Clint held up the now bloody paper towel.

The waitress scrunched her nose, put the plate down on the table in front of him, and hurried off. She was back seconds later with a small roll of white gauze and tape.

"Here," she said and grabbed his hand. "I'm studying to be

a nurse," and as though that was sufficient explanation, she began wrapping his hand with the gauze.

"That's not really necessary," Clint said. She ignored him.

"There," she said as she finished placing a small section of tape over the gauze. She lifted his hand higher and looked at her work. She smiled at him and left to talk to two men at another table.

A couple, possibly in their fifties and wearing coats too heavy for the weather, entered the restaurant and sat at a table next to him. The woman was carrying a large bag from one of the local shops and a handbag.

In seconds, the same waitress that served Clint arrived at their table. The woman at the table did all the talking in a voice that was a little louder than necessary. She and the waitress laughed about something she said. The man with her looked a little uncomfortable.

After the waitress went to get their drinks, the woman said, "Wasn't the canal exquisite. All the small stores and coffee shops." The woman spoke with a strong British accent.

"Yes, dear," her partner said.

The bus tour Clint had taken that morning passed by the canal and the guide recommended everyone visit it. Despite his earlier thought of no more sightseeing, with nothing else planned for the afternoon, he thought he might walk through the canal district. His waitress dropped off the beverages at the table next to him and came by to look at her handy work.

"Yes," she said, after seeing that the bandaging still looked fine.

"What happened?" the woman at the table asked loud enough to be heard at the other end of the room. "Did the wife do that?" She laughed at her own joke.

The waitress looked embarrassed, but Clint lifted his left hand to show all he wasn't married. The waitress gave a slight nod of her head. Clint guessed she wanted him to know she knew he wasn't married, but she didn't want to get involved in the conversation.

"Yes, she's a mean one," Clint said.

The woman laughed even louder. The man with her glanced over at Clint with apologetic eyes.

After that exchange, the couple kept their conversation to themselves. Clint could still hear her, but he ignored what she was saying. His lunch was delicious, and he left a tip equal to the price of the meal. He looked back at his table when he walked out the door and saw his waitress smile and wave to him. She mouthed a thank you.

The walk to the Gran Canal took a half hour. He spent another forty-five minutes meandering from the city end to where the canal opened onto the Adriatic Sea. The abundance of coffee shops, restaurants, and shops did impress him, but Clint did not stop at any of them. Looking down the coast, Clint saw several small and large boat docks and even an industrial area in the harbor. A couple hundred yards off shore he saw a cruise ship.

He heard sirens off in the distance and wondered if someone had discovered the body of the woman.

Chapter 16

"They murdered Henry Dean while he was sitting in that chair a week or two ago. I can't keep up with the days anymore," Melody said.

Kim's hand went to her mouth. "What? Why?"

"We are dealing with some ruthless people. Do not underestimate them. They want us to perfect a small, lethal drone that they can use to kill people or destroy things."

"Why? That makes no sense. They could simply buy a drone to do that," Kim said.

Melody looked at the two men. Maurice took that as an indication she wanted one of them to answer the question.

"We have a couple of theories about that. First, it's hard to buy and use a drone capable of doing that without the drone and the buyer later being identified by a determined security service. Secondly, while some military unit out there may have specialized drones to assassinate people, those type drones would be very hard to acquire. Finally, we're assuming they'll want some specific set of capabilities built into each drone to meet its mission requirements," Maurice said.

Kim looked at all of them like she still couldn't believe what she was hearing.

"It's true, Kim," Melody said.

"And they'll kill us if we don't help them?"

"Only as a last resort, we think," Maurice said.

"They are free with their torture and run-of-the-mill physical cruelty. They will also threaten to harm your family.

We already know they don't mind killing," Melody said.

"They killed my friend," Hideki said.

Kim wondered about her jogging mate.

"Can't we escape?"

"We've all been through that," Melody said.

"And, you should know, they are constantly listening and watching us," Maurice said.

"Have you built one for them yet?" Kim asked. "I mean, once it's done, why would they need us?"

"Good question," Melody said. "We don't actually build the drones. We put together a design, the requirements, etc. If they have built something on what we have given them so far, we haven't seen it. You'll understand in one day how it works."

The door opened, and an armed guard stepped into the room. Maurice could see a second guard outside in the hall.

"Time to get to work. Let's go," the guard motioned with his weapon.

The guards led the four scientists to their lab where they were met by Jack and two of his assistants.

"Please, sit down," Jack said, motioning to the small table in the room.

The four moved to the table.

"We have some good news for you. The initial improvements you recommended helped us with our first test case. Show them," Jack said to one of his assistants.

The assistant sat a laptop down on the table and brought up a short video. The video only ran for about fifteen seconds. At first, no one could figure out what it displayed. The four grouped around to one side, leaned in closer, and watched it again. They watched and saw a man in uniform collapse to the ground. Something very small appeared to fly away as the man fell.

"My God, you killed that man," Maurice said.

"Yes, we did, and we made a nice chunk of money in the process. You don't need to worry about being discovered. Nobody cares about this man. He was just another aspiring warlord in Africa. They have too many already."

"I don't understand," Kim said.

"You don't have to. You only need to work hard and fast. We proved to a major customer what we can do. He now wants our services, and his targets will require much more capable delivery systems. We are making progress, thanks to you three, but we need to move faster. With you here, Dr. Mose, we should be able to meet our goals. Please, get to work." He left the room. His assistant with the laptop followed him.

"Who is he?" Kim whispered.

"We call him Jack, but only to give him a name when we refer to him. We don't know who he or anyone else is here. We don't know where here is either," Melody said.

"He has a rudimentary knowledge of drones, too," Maurice said.

"Did we just see someone really get killed?" Hideki asked.

"It could have been faked, but I believe they are as evil as they imply," Maurice said. From the look on Hideki's face, Maurice thought that the video had really shaken him up. "Don't dwell on it, we may never know if that video was real."

Hideki nodded, but Maurice knew he was still shook-up.

Several hours later in the lab, Maurice thought Kim had grasped enough of what they were doing and how they were doing things to fit right in with the rest of them. Like the others, she questioned why they were using an Israeli drone as their baseline. A question for which none of them had an answer. She also instinctively understood why the team of scientists were providing their captors with small steps to improve the drone rather than jumping right to the state-of-the-art updates.

Late in the day, or night, Maurice really had no idea what time they started or ended their shift, Jack came back in with a blue sheet of paper in his hands.

"Come around the table again."

The four followed his instructions without comment.

"This is what we need to have done in ten days," he said. He handed the paper to Melody.

She looked at it briefly and passed it to Hideki, who sat next to her on her left. He studied the paper for about a minute before passing it on to Maurice. He, in turn, passed it to Kim.

"That is a list of requirements. We have been working to improve the sample drone from the schematics you've provided. The attack on the man in the video was not done by any drone we've been working with," Maurice said.

"So?" Jack said.

"How did anything we provided you assist with the drone used in the video? We could provide better solutions if we knew more about what you're using it on."

"Fair enough. We don't have much time. I'll bring your request up. For now, get to work." Jack left the paper with them and walked out of the lab.

"I thought we didn't really want to help them," Kim whispered.

"We don't. I am very curious, though, with what's really going on. It's been bothering me all day," Maurice said.

"Me, too. They used a miniature drone to attack that man. The drone we've been writing modifications for is twenty times its size," Melody said.

"Maybe they haven't used any of your inputs yet," Kim said.

"That doesn't make sense. All that they have gone through," Maurice said.

"When the Israeli military first designed the drone, they also had a number of prototypes built of various sizes. All were designed about the same but in different sizes. They chose the model we have as our template for a number of reasons, but the schematics for and even a few prototypes of the smallest version could still be out there somewhere," Hideki said, keeping his voice down.

"Some of our modifications would have to be adjusted if they were to be applied to a smaller drone," Maurice said.

"Well, since we don't know if the drone is smaller, that seems to be their problem," Melody said and grinned.

Chapter 17

They left Clint in Trieste for another day before flying him back to Madrid. The body of the dead woman remained undiscovered. Clint resumed his routine of jogging in Retiro Park, followed by a visit to the café in the Plaza Mayor. He rented a car and spent his afternoons and evenings visiting the nearby cities of Segovia and Toledo.

The first contact he had with Section came on the third morning while he was at the café. He had not seen Steffi since his return.

"They found her," Buzz said over the phone.

"Is that good or bad?" Clint knew Buzz referred to the woman in Trieste.

"Mostly good, we think. The immediate response was not to treat it like a crime scene. A lot of people went in and out of the room, and she was moved before they spotted the gun. Even then, the initial theory by the ambulance crew was that she had an accident. They did finally get it sorted, but by then the scene was corrupted."

"Any identification yet?"

"Soon, we hope. They're working fingerprints and DNA right now."

"Am I still on hold here in Madrid?"

"Yes, for the time being, but things could move quickly once she's identified. If she's identified," Buzz said.

Or not, Clint thought. Section didn't learn much from the man he killed in Austria, and the two were working as a team.

He was tempted to ask why they expected to learn anything since they hadn't earlier, but Buzz said he had to run and ended the call.

He took another sip of his coffee and thought again about Deer and her crew. In some ways, he compared her entire operation to a single, small special ops team that had operated in Iraq and the later in Afghanistan. While he was there, he was a member of one of those teams. The team chief would receive intelligence and the targets from some command center, and the team would go out and attack the target.

While the comparison fit well in Clint's mind, he also knew there were a few major differences. First, he knew that Section and its hunters worked completely in the black. And then, although it was hard for Clint to believe, Deer had no real supervisor, no reporting requirements, and supposed complete access to the US intelligence community's data. In addition to the routine shared intelligence, she had the capability to access most of what other agencies collected.

Clint had never filed a report or justified his expenditures. While he had credentials identifying him as being with the US Marshal Service, he had no authority to use them. The couple times he had used them to identify himself at crime scenes, he had to immediately let Section know.

Only a handful of people in the government knew of the existence of Deer's hunters. Buzz had once told him that a handful might be overstating it. Clint imagined one day Section would be shut down, but as long as it was in operation, he was content to be on Deer's team. He didn't know what else he would do, and what would his resume say? His employment history could fit in two lines. He killed people for the military, and afterwards, he killed people for the government. For a variety of reasons, Clint didn't do much dreaming about the future.

Despite the sunshine, a light rain started falling. Clint watched the people in the square hustle to get under some cover or indoors. He didn't see anyone with an umbrella. A few individuals ignored the rain and continued walking to wherever they were going. A cool breeze followed the rain and felt good to Clint. The café's awning, primarily there for shade, kept the rain off him.

Clint ordered a second cup of coffee, thinking he'd give the rain a chance to stop before he moved on. Waiting for the coffee, he saw Steffi walking out of a building across the square with a man. She looked towards Clint but didn't give any sign that she saw him. She and the man walked about twenty yards, staying close to the side of the buildings before entering through another doorway.

His phone buzzed again.

"Clint, I need to you to take another trip," Deer said.

"Okay. Where to?"

"Athens. Mose's kidnapper being in Trieste has lent a little more credence to a theory of mine. A private boat left Trieste the early morning hours on the day after Mose's disappearance. It sailed to Athens. I can't be sure if it stopped somewhere on the way, but it's not far from Trieste to Athens."

"You think that's where they all are?"

"Possibly, but I'm thinking someplace not far from there and a lot more private."

"Anything more on the Kenyan general?" Clint asked.

"Only that the thing that killed him was fairly interesting. They're referring to it as a dart, but I'm not sure how accurate that term is. It was destroyed upon impact, but they're trying to reconstruct it. Upon impact, the dart injected a small dose of a lethal poison. An instant later, the dart explodes."

"How big was this thing?"

"Very small. The explosion may have had no other purpose than to destroy the dart, but it did cause several small lacerations on the general's neck. Whether or not the fragments that cut into his neck as a result of the explosion contained additional poison is unknown right now."

"Seems like an awful complicated way to kill someone."

"Exactly. It's like something you'd see in an old B movie with a mad scientist building this in his basement laboratory. It's not what our missing scientists would come up with."

"Maybe it's not related?"

"No, it's related. I feel it in my bones. I know I don't have to remind you, but if we locate the missing scientists, we'll let the locals do the rescuing."

"I know. Did anyone figure out how the dart was fired?"

"A very small drone, the size of a large dragon fly delivered it and then disappeared. A few people saw it, but no one saw where it went. Its range had to be limited, so the assumption is that someone nearby controlled it."

"Maybe the scientists helped construct the small drone."

"It's possible, but the description of the drone is similar to a few already in existence. They could have helped tweak it, I suppose, and one of our working theories is that whoever kidnapped the scientists want to have the ability to make their own."

Clint thought the discussion had started to go around in circles.

"Do you need me out of here today?"

"No, tomorrow morning should be fine. Buzz will be in touch. We'll better equip you in Athens, and we'll be relocating you there."

"Checking out of this hotel?"

"Yes. Do you have anyone you know in Athens?"

"Yes," Clint said, wondering what he may have said a couple years earlier about Elina Eugeny.

"Good. We'll put you in the Athens Marriott. It's where a lot of American tourists stay, and while it will put you more in the limelight, it is also an obvious place for an American tourist to stay. We'll send you the arrangements shortly."

The call ended. Clint never put much thought into which hotels they booked him into. The small, nice, but out of the way ones, like the one he was booked into in Madrid, were fine by him. A big hotel, like the Marriott in Athens, sounded nice, too.

Chapter 18

"You have used up all your good will. Last week my boss was pleased, but now he is getting impatient," Jack said.

The four scientists stood together in the lab. They had only been brought there a few minutes before.

"I don't set the timetable. He does, and when we fall behind, he gets mad. He frightens me when he gets mad, and I don't frighten easily. We will meet the deadline or Hideki will get to sit in Dean's chair for real. You want that to happen?"

"Of course not," Maurice said.

Jack looked at him, studying his face before turning his attention to Melody.

"I thought you spoke for the group. Is he in charge now?"

"We work together as a team. The only boss in the room is you," Melody said.

"Good attitude, and you're right. I am the only boss you four have." He grinned and looked back at Hideki. "You are a dead man if we don't get the boss what he wants."

"We will do our best, but we don't know enough about what you are trying to do. We can give you ways to enhance the drone's speed, range, and load capacity, but those will always be general recommendations. Without knowing the exact mission, the exact drone, and everything else, we may be providing you good recommendations but for the wrong system or mission," Melody said.

"She is right, you know. I've only been here a short time,

but I've wondered what good our recommendations are? Without seeing the results of our recommendations, we don't know if the recommendations we've provided need to be tweaked," Kim said. Her frustration resonated in her voice.

"I will talk to my boss. I understand your position, I have discussed this with him before, so I can make no promises." Jack moved closer to Kim. "You don't talk to me in that tone again, or I will personally teach you some manners."

"We're all stressed. She didn't mean anything," Melody said.

"Work harder. I'll be back to help this afternoon," Jack said and left the lab. The other lab technician who had arrived with him moved to a console across the room and fiddled with a panel for a few minutes before leaving the room, too.

"I didn't mean to anger him," Kim said.

"How can we be sure what we provide them is what they need? They are going to kill me, aren't they?" Hideki pressed his fingers against his forehead.

"No, I think that was to get us motivated," Maurice said, not believing his statement at all. Their captors had no qualms about killing any of them.

"Kim, what you said to Jack, he knows it's true. It shouldn't have angered him, and I doubt if he'd be the one that would, as he said, teach you some manners. I think he is under a lot of pressure, too. His boss is the evil man," Melody said.

"Did he –"

"Yes. There will be nothing you can do to defend yourself."

"I will kill him first," Kim whispered.

"I hope you do, but just prepare yourself not to let it affect your mind. Only the strong survive here," Melody said. A few seconds after she said this, she turned her face toward Hideki.

Maurice hoped Hideki understood her remark targeted him as well as Kim.

"We all need to be here for each other," Maurice said. He didn't know exactly what Melody had gone through, but he remembered seeing her bruises when he met her and imagined it wasn't pleasant.

Maurice suggested they all sit down at the table and discuss a theory Hideki had mentioned. He had two reasons for making the recommendation. First, Hideki's idea seemed simple enough and would likely increase the range of the drone. Second, and perhaps more important at the moment, Maurice wanted to get Hideki refocused on their work and away from any thoughts of imminent death.

They all agreed. Melody looked at Maurice and gave him an almost imperceptible nod. Maurice took this as a sign that she, too, thought they needed to get Hideki back into the game.

After spending thirty minutes analyzing the idea, Hideki took the lead at a nearby computer and ran the modifications through the simulator software. The other three stood behind him watching.

"Yes, see that," Hideki said, pointing to the screen.

"It's small, but it is an improvement. Is this your original theory? It's brilliantly simple, yet I've never heard it before," Kim said.

"Very good," Melody said.

"Yes. My friend, Sache, came up with it, and we had tinkered with it for a while, but it had never gotten off the back burner. We were always too busy."

"Sache, he was killed when they took you," Kim said.

"Yes. I saw it. I knew I saw it," Hideki said.

"How do you know?" Maurice asked.

"You've all been on the news. I was even visited by my country's security personnel and warned to be cautious. Little good it did me. I wonder if they killed my friend?" Kim said.

"Don't dwell on that. It will do you no good," Maurice said.

"Someone else showed up. I don't know who he was. Maybe he saved my friend."

"What do you mean?" Hideki asked.

"Two people attacked us. A man and a woman."

"That was the same for me," Hideki said.

"I tried to run away, but the woman chased me. The man and my friend began fighting, but I didn't see much of it. I kept running. The woman ran faster and shot me with a tranquilizer dart."

"She shot me with one, too. What about this other man?" Maurice asked.

"I didn't see him clearly. The drug didn't have its full effect with me, or maybe it was designed that way, so I didn't have to be carried. I felt like I was sleepwalking. I had no willpower to wake up or resist. Must be like one of those rape date drugs that I have fortunately never experienced."

"But you remember this?" Melody asked.

"Not all. To be honest I may have imagined some, but I remember being in the trees and seeing this man I never saw before running along the path. I felt like he was looking for me. I can't explain it. The woman swore something. She tried calling someone but got no answer. She swore again, and then we started walking away. I don't remember much more until I heard the car trunk being shut, and I found myself in it."

"I don't remember anything after being drugged," Hideki said.

Maurice wanted to say, "Me, too," but kept silent. He wanted Kim to continue.

"I was half unconscious, but I heard her outside the car talking. I think she was on a phone. She was saying someone was missing or hadn't come yet. He wasn't answering her calls. She wanted to know what she should do. I sensed she didn't like the answer, but moments later we drove off. After that, I can't remember anything either."

"We all hope someone is looking for us," Maurice said.

"They are," Kim said.

"I wish we had access to the news," Maurice said. Kim's confidence that there were people looking for them comforted him. While he had always thought there would be, Kim had access to the news after they had all been kidnapped. She had also been cautioned by her country's security service. Her saying they were being searched for was all the proof he needed.

Jack entered the room carrying a laptop and followed by a guard.

"Put your chairs on one side of the table. I have something to show you," he said.

"What is it?" Melody asked.

"Be patient. I've been authorized to show you this. However, my boss also said if you find any reason to stall your efforts after seeing this, you will be killed Hideki, and we will send a team out to kill your family, Maurice. There will be no warnings," Jack said.

"You will kill us anyway when you are done with us," Kim said.

"Why? You know none of us. You don't know where you are, and each of you will be as complicit as I am. Besides, we would not kill a woman. The boss says there is always a market out there for a woman. Places they can be taken to and never reappear. Terrible places."

"You wouldn't," Maurice said.

"How innocent you are, Maurice. Don't you worry. There is no market for old men. Now, unless someone else wants to risk their sleep tonight, pay attention."

Jack brought something up on the computer screen and turned it around so everyone could see it. He clicked on the screen and a video started.

Maurice recognized the display as a commercial marketing video produced by some company trying to sell small drones to a nation's military. The video started with two small drones taking off from a field and begin tracking toward a jeep driving down a dirt path in the distance. After about thirty seconds the drones closed in on the jeep and each fired a small rocket that destroyed the jeep.

"Are those drones ones you've enhanced by our inputs? Melody asked.

Maurice hadn't thought of that.

"No, but these two drones are smaller modified versions of the drone you've been using as our prototype. These smaller drones are the ones we will be using as a template to build our own."

"You know everything we've provided you so far was for the larger model. Many of our recommendations have to be reworked. Your boss has set you and us up for failure," Melody said.

Instead of getting agitated, Jack smiled. "I know. Now he does."

"Good," Hideki said. "I don't want to be killed for failing the wrong test."

"You are not off the hook," Jack said.

"You'll see. We will provide better recommendations now that we know what we are dealing with," Melody said.

"One more thing, and do pay attention. This may be the critical piece." He started a different video.

Maurice again believed he was watching an advertisement. A very small drone, the size of a hummingbird, flew off the top of a table. It flew directly against a target on a wall some twenty to thirty feet away where it exploded on contact. The explosion did not seem significant, but like a firecracker it could severely harm a human target.

"I know that drone," Hideki said.

"Yes, your knowledge of miniaturization is why we selected you. We need this template to be enhanced, too. We need more range, carrying capacity, and perhaps smaller size."

"You need to give us the specs for these, um, your templates," Melody said.

"I'll get them to you today," he said and started walking out of the room carrying the laptop. He paused at the door. "Kim, my boss is not impressed with your effort." Jack left, but two of his unnamed lab technicians stayed behind.

Chapter 19

Jack did not return with the specs for the templates of the drones they wanted enhanced until the next day. He entered the lab a few minutes after the four scientists arrived. He put his briefcase on the table and from it, he removed one sheet of folded paper. Unfolding it, Jack placed it on the table for all to see. The page displayed the schematics of the Israeli Hero 30 drone, a small drone in use by Israel and a few other countries' military services.

"We want this modified. Smaller, better range, and keep the load capability the same or better."

"How soon?" Melody asked.

"Five days. We need time to make the changes and test the drone."

"You make it here?" Kim asked.

"Do not worry about that," Jack said.

"It would help us if we knew what the drone will be used for," Maurice asked.

"Of course," Jack said. He retrieved a laptop from his briefcase, opened it, and turned it on.

All four scientists gathered around Jack to get a better view of the laptop. Maurice noticed one of the guards put his hand on his holstered pistol.

"Watch," Jack said and took a step back to allow the scientists a better view.

Maurice had a hard time understanding what he was supposed to see. The only thing displayed on the screen looked like a wooden utility pole. An electric transformer, attached to the pole, appeared to be the main focus of the camera. Trees were in the background, but nothing gave Maurice any idea where or when the video was made.

Suddenly, something flew through the air and struck the transformer, causing it to explode. The explosion did sufficient damage to the transformer to cause it to shoot sparks out in all direction. He replayed the video at a slower speed.

"One dead transformer," Jack said. He closed the cover of the laptop and placed it back in the briefcase.

"All this is just to destroy transformers?" Maurice asked, instantly regretting the sarcasm in his voice.

"We have our reasons," Jack said. He stared at Maurice until Maurice looked down in an obvious display of subservience.

After Jack and the others left, Melody leaned in close to Maurice. "Be careful."

"Why do they need us if they only want to go after transformers?" Hideki asked.

"Let's not worry about that. We need to get to work. Most all of our prior recommendations need to be adjusted," Melody said.

"So, we start over," Maurice said.

"Not entirely, look closely here," Melody said, and they all leaned in close to the paper Jack left on the table.

"I don't believe transformers are their target, either, Hideki," Melody whispered. "But what does it matter? Let's work with what we have and pray that no one gets hurt from what we do."

Maurice leaned back out of the group and spoke loud

enough for everyone to hear. "I agree, they must be wanting to blackmail companies or even countries by knocking out the grid."

"To be clear, what they want us to do is help them reverse engineer existing drones. They want them smaller, more efficient, and more deadly," Kim said.

"Very well put," Melody said. "Most all drones are moving in that direction already. For some reason, money most likely, these guys want one of their own now."

"We should get some of the royalties," Maurice said.

"You know," Hideki said and paused for a second.

"What?" Maurice asked.

"The drone that hit the transformer was very small. We should have clarified if the drone we are supposed to build is the one that hit the transformer or the one that delivers it to the target area."

Melody looked at Hideki with her eyes scrunched. "Good point. The drone we just watched was nothing like the second template we were given. We have also been led to believe the drones had fired small rockets."

"Could they want us to build a much smaller version of the template to use in the same fashion? I mean the drone we watched has to have very limited range. As small as it was and carrying a payload capable of such destruction, how far could it travel?" Kim said.

"Plus, it had to have a targeting system. It has to be able to acquire and hit its target. Several models have that capability, but that adds weight and size to the drone. Cuts down on range," Hideki said.

"And that was a drone," Maurice said. "I mean it wasn't just a projectile being fired from something offsite."

"No, it was a drone," Kim said.

"We may be overthinking this. They want us to work off their templates, and they now want us to design a drone that can do what we saw on the monitor. A smaller version of their earlier template for sure, but with more range and capability than the drone we watched. Maybe they wanted our drone to deliver that killer drone to the target site. Now, they may want us to enhance the killer drone. It would give them the ability to stay far away from their target while executing whatever transformer they want to kill," Melody said.

"You're right, Melody. We may never know exactly how they want to use our information. That may be a good thing. We might not want to know," Hideki said.

"So, we design this thing smaller, with more range, and with the capability to deliver a payload to a target. We all knew the payload could be another drone or an explosive. Now maybe we're enhancing the much smaller killer drone," Maurice said.

"And one or both with a long-range guidance system," Kim said. "There are a number of them we could recommend. First, we had small drones, then mini-drones, and now we have nano-drones. The science for all is related and not new."

"You're right. Let's not over think this," Melody said.

"I agree. They obviously have the ability to manufacture a drone. They could simply reverse engineer an existing one, but they seem to want to have an enhanced version of whatever drone they make. Better and different," Maurice said.

"By tweaking it with our modifications. I think they do want them to be unique, so they can't be traced," Hideki said.

They all nodded in agreement and started discussing different approaches.

Fifteen minutes later, the lab door opened, and Jack walked in carrying a crystal carafe of red wine and five crystal wine glasses.

"Let's take a ten-minute break. We've made progress today, so I thought we could celebrate." He set the wine on a small table in the corner and proceeded to pour and pass out the wine glasses.

"A toast to our successful accomplishment, and your safe return to your families," he said.

Maurice almost choked and fought the urge to throw the glass at him. He saw Hideki's hands tremble and knew he felt the same way.

"Thank you for the wine. You must know that none of us are thrilled with the position you've put us in; however, let's all agree that we have our sights on the end goal. We all look forward to going home," Melody said. She tapped her glass against Jack's before tapping each of the others.

In doing so, she stared into the eyes of each of her fellow scientists with what Maurice interpreted as a plea not to do anything stupid.

"A good wine, what is it?" Melody asked.

"A local wine, one of my favorites," Jack said. "Now I must leave, and you must get back to work. I believe you all are on the right track now."

Melody changed the topic. "To clarify, you want us to work on the delivery drone, not the smaller drone, or was that a rocket?"

"We have taken some of your inputs and used them on

both. Our main goal is to increase the efficiency of the larger of the two. The delivery drone, as you say. We want it smaller and with better range."

They watched him walk out. Only one lab technician remained in the room, but he kept himself in the far corner with his back to them.

"That was surreal," Maurice said.

"I wanted to scream at him," Hideki whispered.

"I'm glad you didn't," Melody said as softly. "We learned something today. I believe this is a Greek wine." She sipped the wine again.

Kim took another sip and, looking at Melody, nodded. "You may be correct."

"We're in Greece?" Maurice said.

Hideki had to lean in close to hear him.

"If it's a local wine," Melody said.

"Well, at least we got some clarification. I guess we should get back to work," Maurice said in a louder voice. He couldn't tell a Cabernet Sauvignon from a Merlot, much less tell a Greek wine from a California wine, yet he knew there were those who could.

Chapter 20

The Athens Marriott made Clint's boutique hotel in Madrid look like a hideaway. Crammed into a congested setting, parked cars squeezed against each other along the curb surrounding the hotel. Taxis lined the front entrance, and people seemed to be coming and going all the time. Twice since his arrival the day before, he had to avoid a group of young adults rushing into or out of the hotel.

The hotel inside presented a different picture with all the amenities of the upscale hotel chain. A nice bar area decorated the center of the lobby. The three wings of the hotel surrounded a private outdoor courtyard that could be reached via the bar or the restaurant. Clint's seventh floor room gave him a decent, partial view of the city.

He had planned to spend his first few days walking around the city, but a cold front had settled over southern Greece, and a persistent light rain kept him mostly indoors. He had taken a taxi to the Acropolis Museum on his second day and spent half the day there. He also walked two city blocks to a restaurant recommended by the hotel's concierge. The dinner did not disappoint him.

Clint's phone had remained quiet. Usually, that didn't bother him. He had learned from his time in the military, as well as working for Deer, that a lot of the job required sitting around waiting. He imagined that was the same for firemen, policemen, and even life guards.

"Life guards," he said out loud to himself, wondering why

they popped into his mind. They did fit, though, as they, too, sat watching for hours on end before jumping up to make the occasional rescue.

Here in Athens, however, the lack of activity did start to bother him as he intended to contact Elina once he completed his mission, or Deer called it off. At least the next day's weather report called for sunshine.

The day turned out sunny as predicted. Clint finished his glass of Mythos and ordered another. He estimated he had walked five miles today. The hike up to the Parthenon had been the toughest part, but he had enjoyed it. He tried to imagine what it would've been like two thousand years earlier. A rough life, for sure, and a period of time Clint was happy he didn't have to experience. Cher brought him his second glass of beer and sat down beside him.

"It's Cher, like the American singer," she had said to him two days earlier on his first visit to the taverna.

"You're much prettier than her," Clint had replied.

"Bah! Don't be silly," Cher responded but smiled as she walked away. A few minutes later, she approached him again. "Business is always slow at five o'clock in the afternoon. You must be a tourist."

"Guilty. I've always wanted to visit Athens. Is this your taverna?"

"Mine? I wish. No, my uncle is the owner. It's been in my mother's family for over fifty years. She worked here as a young girl."

Cher said it with pride. Clint liked her. Tall, thin with jet black hair worn in a pony tail, she spent most of her time working hard, cleaning and dusting the entire room. She spoke fluent English. During that first visit, she stopped her constant cleaning and talked to him briefly three times.

As he stood up from the small table to leave, she hurried over to him. "Thank you. I hope you have a nice time in our city," she said.

"Do you work here every afternoon?"

"Yes, but not on weekends."

"Then I might see you tomorrow," Clint said.

"Yes," she said and smiled.

True to his word, Clint returned in the late afternoon. On this day, the restaurant was as empty, and Cher spent several minutes leaning against an adjacent table talking to Clint.

Eventually, she took the seat next to him. "What did you do today?"

"Touristy things. I visited the Parthenon. Did a lot of walking."

"Alone?"

"Unfortunately."

"Are you going to be here Saturday?"

"It looks like it."

She studied him for a second. Clint thought she was trying to decide what he meant and why he didn't know.

"If you are, I would be happy to show you the best parts of Athens most tourists never visit," she said.

"I would love that, but are you sure you want to spend your day off with me?"

"If I get too bored, I can cut the tour short. After all, I'll be the tour guide," she said.

"My treat, though, I put aside enough money for this vacation to have at least one nice excursion."

"It won't be expensive," she laughed.

She sat next to him for another five minutes before four men entered the taverna.

"Some more early birds. I bet they're American businessmen. No sensible Greek would come this early," she laughed at her own comment and strolled off to greet the four men.

The new arrivals kept her busy. Clint finished his beer and left, waving to her as he went out the door. He already looked forward to Saturday. Doing nothing but "keeping a low profile" in Athens had started to annoy him. Back in his hotel room, his phone buzzed.

"Hey, Clint, how's it going?" Buzz asked.

"A bit boring, I think I've walked the entire city already."

"Unfortunately, it's been the same here. The whole world has quieted down, except for the Russian invasion of Ukraine. That's been keeping the rest of the community busy but has nothing to do with us."

"How's Deer handling it?"

"Outwardly calm, but I believe she's quite anxious for something else to pop."

"Think something will?"

"Most definitely. She wants to keep you there for a while. I'm not sure if that means a few more days or weeks."

"Okay," Clint said, not really knowing what he wanted to say about the idea of staying here for weeks. "Let's hope something happens sooner rather than later."

"If something pops, we'll let you know," Buzz said and ended the call.

Chapter 21

"Sit down, Efran. We're going to get a live view of our next test. By the way, I may start calling you Jack. It makes me think of you more like how I think of our guest scientists. That way if you disappoint me, I can treat you like one of them."

Efran shuddered as he sat down next to his boss, Sonder Agape. He considered Sonder a sociopath. His recent murder of Henry Dean in front of his fellow scientists was only the most recent example. Efran considered what Sonder had done to Melody Spencer sadistic. He had forced Efran to watch.

"Okay," Sonder said to a young man sitting in front of a computer.

The man clicked on a few keys, and large screen in front of them came to life with a view from what Efran knew must be a drone in the air.

"We have a few minutes. Our target is a bus carrying some Israeli athletes to some event somewhere in France. I'm not being secretive, it's simply that I don't care. I only care that it's a successful mission. Our customer must have his reasons, but they're irrelevant to me."

"It should work, sir," Efran said. A bead of sweat rolled down his forehead into his right eye. He wiped his sleeve across his face.

"There," Sonder said, pointing at the screen.

Efran knew he was watching a live, video feed from a drone. Their drone, he guessed. He could see a bus in the distance, still over a mile from the drone. The drone, flying fast, quickly closed the distance. Suddenly, the drone's nose shot upward.

"What the hell!"

"No, it's okay," Efran said. The drone settled, and both men saw the bus come back into view. They saw what appeared to be a dark dart flying toward the bus at amazing speed, impacting with the bus in a few seconds. The front of the bus exploded. The explosion seemed rather small, but the bus swerved off the road, colliding with a large tree. The screen turned black.

"Our drone will now be returning. It will travel at top speed and take evasive action as necessary. A self-destruct capability is built into it, too."

"Yes, yes, I know all that," Sonder said. "You know, I felt like breaking your kneecaps the other day when I heard you were drinking wine with the scientists. Now, however, I feel like breaking out the champagne."

"Should I?"

"No. Don't waste any on them. You will get a bonus, of course. That little test mission will bring in a substantial payment. Ten times that much will come in with the next step. If all things are working at that point, we will be killing your male pets and selling off the two women, so don't get too attached."

"Can I tell them that we have tested the new drones, and they are working fine."

"Yes, yes, something like that," Sonder said. "Have they figured out they are helping us with both the delivery and the terminal drones?"

"They might. I have deliberately tried to confuse them, just a little. They have questions about which one are they doing, but I do not believe they know. I told them to focus on the delivery drone for now."

"By the way, I was thinking of letting you break in the new one. You know, the way I did the first woman."

"I don't think we should, sir. With all respect, the team has good momentum, and we are so close."

"Hmm. Maybe you're right. When we're done with them, and if we are successful, you can have her until we firm up a buyer for the two. You may go."

Efran left the briefing room. He didn't relax until he stepped into the elevators at the other end of the building. He hadn't become attached to the scientists, but he hated any forms of torture. The stories of what the Russian soldiers did to his grandmother and other gypsies at the end of World War II had sickened him his whole life.

In fact, Efran still blamed that incident for his current lot in life. His grandmother's sister took his mother with her as she escaped the violence, fleeing south to Greece. His grandfather joined them later and fell in with a band of smugglers and petty thieves. That legacy continued with his father and then with him.

Sonder had taken over the small but powerful crime family that had drafted Efran into its lot. Efran had hopes of becoming legitimate. He went to college, the first in his family to do so, getting a degree in mechanical engineering. Returning home to Thessaloniki, Greece, was his mistake. Once back here, the crime family put him to work repairing stolen items. All types of items: car engines, clocks, boat engines, even an airplane. He tried to explain he wasn't a mechanic, but no one cared.

The unfortunate reality for him was that he was good at it. He gained status, and unfortunately, the eye of Sonder Agape. Efran had worked on a number of special projects for Sonder, but nothing like this before. He didn't know who had hired Sonder for this current project. He didn't care, and he believed the less he knew the better. Sonder's vicious reputation included his murdering many of his own lieutenants for nothing more than "possibly" leaking information.

While he didn't know what the next target or targets would be, Efran was curious. He understood the purpose behind making their own drones. He had assured Sonder the drones would be untraceable. He believed them to be as sophisticated as any that could be purchased on the open market and better than what many nations' militaries have.

It wouldn't be that hard. Sonder owned the company that manufactured drones for sale to individuals and non-military organizations. A large market existed for them both as sophisticated toys for the general population and as useful tools for many companies. The plant took up most of the large building they occupied.

Efran knew the drones the scientists were helping them design would be used to kill people and destroy things. While he would rather not be doing this, the killing no longer bothered him. He had been around murder for most of his adult life, although he had never killed anyone. Indirectly, he had helped in the murder of others. This project was a good example, but being in the business of killing was different than doing it yourself. Anyone who builds fighter jets or battleships knows this.

The elevator door opened.

Chapter 22

Clint rolled over in his bed and reached for his phone. He shook his head and rubbed his face, trying to clear his mind. He glanced at the phone and saw that he had only been asleep for a few minutes.

"Hello."

"We had another drone attack," Buzz said.

"Where? When?" Clint asked.

"This morning, just outside Paris."

"Related to what I'm on?" He realized it was a stupid question as soon as it came out of his mouth.

"Deer is sure of it. Took a few hours for the locals to piece it together. The driver and four passengers were killed. Many of the others were injured. A few were sure they saw what they thought was a small drone impact with the windshield right in front of the driver. A passenger in the back thought he saw a drone flying away in the distance a few seconds after the impact.

"Who were they?"

"Israeli athletes. Deer believes this was a test. There are several countries who might target the Israelis. Too easy to accept the motivation for the attack. It messes up any inquiry, and no one of any significance was on the bus. I don't mean their lives don't matter," Buzz said.

"A killer drone."

"Yes, and most modern militaries have access to them. The French will be analyzing any fragments they can find to try to identify the drone, but we think they won't have much luck."

"This should really get the intelligence community focused."

"They already are. CIA and NSA are all over it. The French and other European countries are, too. The Israelis, obviously, are, and they're likely to retaliate blindly."

"Understandable. Are you sure that whoever is doing this doesn't simply want another Mideast war?"

"Deer seems to be. However, it's something we have considered."

"What do you mean when you call it a test?"

"She thinks this was a practice run. A target of opportunity to test out their capability and maybe to prove to their customer they can deliver. The bus was not guarded. It was on a well-traveled route, and a simple road side bomb could have done as much damage."

"Any change to my status?"

"Not yet, but she seems to think something will develop soon, and, you know, she's often right. We'll keep you posted."

The call ended, and Clint found himself wide awake. He switched on the television and watched a BBC show about food preparation in the Himalayas. In twenty minutes, he was back asleep.

The sound of someone on the television laughing woke him. Sunlight invaded the room through breaks in the curtains. Looking at his watch, Clint saw that he had slept until eight thirty. He found an English-speaking news channel on the television. After a brief talk about the latest World Cup results, the announcer brought up the attack on the Israeli athletes.

The news identified the dead athletes and described the

route the bus had taken. The male newscaster claimed the French authorities were working several leads but were not prepared to make any statements about the perpetrators, the motive, or how that attack was carried out. Despite this, he stated that several unofficial sources said the bus had been attacked by a drone. He then brought up the attack on Israeli athletes in Munich decades before and introduced a professor who was supposedly an expert on Middle Eastern conflicts. The professor opined that one of the more aggressive middle eastern factions were likely behind the attack.

The news report ended with the announcer saying that no group had yet claimed responsibility for the attack.

Clint turned the television off. He got dressed and went down to the hotel's restaurant. A large breakfast buffet had attracted most of the hotel's population, so Clint found an empty, small table in the adjacent bar area. The hotel's management must have seen the need for this overflow area and had situated a coffee station on the bar's counter. An employee of the hotel, a woman with black hair no longer than his, recognized him and came over to him.

"Good morning, can I get you a croissant?" she asked. She had seen him fight the line to get a single croissant a couple of days earlier. Yesterday she had offered and brought one to him. Getting access through the employee side of the buffet had its benefits.

"Yes, please," he said. He watched her walk off. She had a slight limp with her left leg, and a long scar traveled from her left wrist to her elbow. He guessed she was close to fifty years old. While the scar was an old one and somewhat faded, it was still visible. The fact that she chose to wear a short sleeve blouse despite the scar impressed him. Her eyes also intrigued him. They were green, and he couldn't think of another person he had seen in Athens with green eyes.

She returned moments later with the croissant. He had already poured himself a coffee.

"Anything else?"

"No, thank you. Is this hotel always so busy?"

"Most of the time. It's a Marriott," she said, as if that should explain it.

"Have you lived here in Athens your whole life?"

"No. I was born in Lebanon, but my family moved here when I was eleven. Too many wars," she held up her arm, displaying the scar.

Clint nodded. He had witnessed some of fighting first hand, not in Lebanon, but in the region.

"Why do you ask?"

"No reason, really, I was just curious."

She smiled at him and walked away.

He had wanted to ask her another question. Her name tag identified her as Tish. He figured it was a nickname, but he couldn't come up with a name from which it might have come. His phone interrupted his thoughts.

"How are you doing, Clint?" Deer asked.

"Fine," he said, although he almost said bored. He wondered what had Deer awake at what must be the middle of the night in D.C.

"I need you to check something out for me. I have a GPS location, and I'd like you to take a look at what's there. I've checked Google maps and a few other online mapping sites, but all I can get is an aerial shot. It's no good."

"No street address?"

"Not that I have. It's the sight of a server that has received a handful of messages I believe are linked to this. By good fortune, it's on the outskirts of Athens."

"Want me to enter the place?" Clint asked.

"No, no. I want you to get a picture or two of it from the street and get the street address, or at least the street that it's on."

"I can do it. My calendar is free today."

"It's not something I can simply share with the Greeks or even someone here. I had to get this data on my own."

"Not a problem. I'll go by there today."

"Thanks," Deer said and ended the call.

Clint knew what she meant when she said she had to get the GPS location on her own. Section, her small agency, had backdoor access to most, if not all, of the US Intelligence Community databases. Clint believed these other agencies had no idea Deer had such access, so going back to them with their own data that had not been shared could cause quite the uproar. Buzz had explained to him that this access was approved when Section was created. Like everything else with Section, only a few people knew about this or anything else that pertained to Section. Over the years since its creation, most of those individuals had retired or died.

A text message came in with nothing else but a series of numbers. Clint copied the numbers and put it in as a GPS location. A map appeared on his phone. He studied it and identified a nearby location that might serve as a spot a lonely, bored tourist might want to visit.

Chapter 23

Clint found a cab driver in front of the hotel, whom he could hire for the morning. The set fee seemed high to Clint, but he accepted it with a comment that he expected first class treatment for that amount.

"Why, of course, sir," the driver replied.

"Pasho?" Clint asked, reading the embroidered name on the man's shirt.

"That's what they call me." The driver had a big grin that reminded Clint of a used car salesman he encountered on occasion at the firing range back on South Padre Island.

"I'm expecting some friends this weekend, and I'd like to checkout Voula Beach. There are also one or two other stops I'd like to make."

"That should be easy, sir. When would you like to leave?"

"In about fifteen minutes."

"Yes, sir."

"Please call me Clint. I need to run back to my room, then I'll be down."

The drive to the beach did not take long. Clint had chosen it because of its proximity to the city center, and because the location he really wanted to check out was nearby. He spent a couple of minutes outside the cab pretending to study the beach and its amenities. He took a number of pictures with his phone and then studied his phone like he was looking at the pictures. Instead, he pulled up the map of the area, pinpointing the location of the target Deer had given him.

Earlier, he found an old Greek Orthodox church that the online tour guides listed as a secondary level church that might be of interest to the most serious fans of old churches. He had already studied the map and estimated the target location to be less than a half kilometer from the church. His plan had him telling the cab driver that he might be in the church for fifteen minutes to a half hour. That would give him ample time to circle back and get a picture or two of his target. However, like a lot of plans, it quickly became overcome by events.

By chance, the drive to the church took him down the street on which his target was located.

"This is not a good part of Athens," Pasho said. He slowed down to avoid some young men strolling down the middle of the road.

They stared at the taxi as it went by. Clint imagined they were sizing it up and decided a taxi held little interest for them. Two elderly women dressed in all black sat on lawn chairs, smoking, near the front of another small house. There was no grass on the front yard. An old apartment building with broken windows that seemed abandoned took up most of a block outside the left side of the taxi.

"Sorry to make you bring me here. I didn't know," Clint said.

"I should have, but I haven't been down here in a long time. Dekara!" Pasho cursed.

A person had staggered backwards into the street, and Pasho slammed on the brakes. The man had been hidden in front of a small truck parked on the side of the road. Two more men stepped out from in front of the truck and grabbed the first man. One of the two slapped the first man in the face.

Pasho made a tactical mistake and honked at the men. The two men looked at Pasho, and Pasho raised both hands in a gesture Clint interpreted to mean "what's going on?" or "why are you in the road?"

While Clint did not think Pasho's gesture was particularly aggressive, one of the two men must have felt otherwise. He marched around to the driver's door, yanking it open. Pasho and the man started yelling at each other in Greek. The man tried to yank Pasho out of the car. None of the men held any sort of weapon in their hands, so Clint decided to take advantage of the diversion. Studying his phone, he realized that the GPS location Deer had sent to him matched the location of a small house that sat at the edge of the apartment building. Barely three feet of dirt and weeds separated the house from the larger building.

The house looked poorly maintained, but there was a motorcycle parked in front of it. He had a fairly good view of the house, so Clint snapped a picture of it. He had slid his phone back into his pocket when the second man ran over to his passenger side window and banged his fist against it.

He started yelling at Clint in Greek, getting everyone's attention. Pasho and the man who had confronted him had about argued themselves out.

Pasho turned to Clint and said, "He's saying you took his friend's picture."

"No, I didn't," Clint said, keeping his voice calm. He checked to make sure the door was locked.

The man who had been yelling at Pasho moved around to Clint's side of the taxi and yelled something in Greek at Clint.

"He wants your phone," Pasho said.

"I'm not giving it to him."

With both men now focused on Clint, Pasho closed his door and drove off, leaving the two men standing there. The third man, whom the two had assaulted, had already left. Clint could see him running away.

"Well, that was exciting," Clint said.

Pasho murmured something to himself in his native language. They reached the church in less than a minute, and Pasho drove the taxi around to the opposite side of the church before coming to a stop.

"That was bad. They wanted to fight us," Pasho said. "I need to call that into my company."

"Do you know the address?"

"It was on Mascos. I don't know the number, but it was a half kilometer from this church. The police should know the area."

"It was right next to that apartment building that looked abandoned."

"Yes, that's right."

"We're not going back there, are we?" Clint asked, feigning apprehension.

"No, I will ask my company to report it to the police. Do you still want to go into this church?" Pasho looked around while he spoke. Then before waiting for an answer, he called what Clint believed to be someone in the taxi company on his phone. While Clint didn't understand what Pasho said, he could hear the excitement in his voice and see the gestures he used with his free hand.

Adrenalin, Clint thought. He remained in the car and sent a text with the picture of the small house to Buzz. "Target is a small house on Mascos Street, East side, a half kilometer from the Little Church of God. Not sure what the actual Greek name is for the church." He had not received a response by the time Pasho had ended his call.

"They will contact the police. Do you want to go inside?"

"No, it's too close to those guys, and I think I want to go back to the hotel. I will still pay you the fee I promised."

"I understand."

Clint believed the incident had shaken Pasho, while it gave Clint a good excuse to return to the hotel. Both of the men who had confronted them looked like rough characters, but barring the sudden appearance of some weapon, Clint had not viewed either as much of a physical threat.

Back at the hotel, Pasho surprised Clint by trying to turn down any payment. Clint insisted, saying he had cancelled the rest of the morning. It was not Pasho's fault. Plus, he thought he might want to use Pasho again in the future.

The phone call from Buzz came in a few minutes later. Clint had made himself a cup of coffee in his room and was sitting out on the room's small balcony. From his seventh-floor vantage point he could see a good portion of the large city.

"We received your text," Buzz said.

"Not sure what good it will do you."

"Not much for me, but she likes to get a good feel for things. I think it helps her visualize her theories, and you know, she is phenomenally good at it."

Clint did know.

Chapter 24

The air always seemed to be fresher down here. Three levels below the surface, Efran, or Jack as the scientists called him, knew the air was recycled. Still, the air here was a pleasant change from the toxic atmosphere in Sonder's office.

In Efran's dreams, he had on occasion envisioned Sonder as one of Satan's demons, fouling everything close to him. He once dreamed he died and went to hell, only to discover he still had to work for Sonder when they were both in hell. A silly thought, he knew, but it bothered him.

He walked down a short hallway and entered the lab. The four scientists sat at their work table with a printout of something. They appeared to be in agreement.

They all glanced at him as he entered. Their eyes showed no fear of him, and that pleased Efran. Truth be told, he'd rather befriend these four than have them killed, but he could do nothing about it.

"Another breakthrough?" he asked.

"A small one," Hideki said.

"That is good. The boss wanted me to let you know he is pleased with your effort. We have put it through a second test with excellent results. However, he still wants more range without increasing the size or weight."

"Should we still be working off the schematics you showed us? If not, could you bring us the schematics of the actual drone you are using, we could do a much better and quicker job at providing you solutions," Melody said.

"I know, and now that we are close to being done, I'll ask him again."

"Does this mean we might be released fairly soon?" Kim asked.

"Perhaps, but that, too, is out of my hands. Now tell me, what have you come up with today?"

Hideki started to explain what they had been discussing.

"One second," Efran said and raised his hand, gesturing with his palm to Hideki. "Was this your discovery? Is that why you're doing the talking?"

Hideki looked toward Melody. She nodded.

"Yes, it was something that I thought of last night," Hideki said.

"Excellent."

He stayed and listened to Hideki's recommendation. It made sense. He congratulated them all again before leaving.

Going back to his small office on the same level as the lab, he was surprised to see Eddy standing in the hall by his door. Eddy had always frightened him. Eddy frightened everybody. He towered over Efran. From the stories he had heard, Efran believed Eddy had been a vicious bully his whole life. At the age of twelve, he had allegedly killed a neighbor boy when the boy made the mistake of trying to steal Eddy's bike. The stories about him only got worse as he grew older.

Sonder scared Efran, and Sonder could kill someone without a bit of remorse, but the most frightening thing about Sonder was Eddy. Eddy was his pit bull. Sonder had many other killers working for him, but none of them were as terrifying as Eddy. He had come from somewhere in the Balkans as a teenager. Eddy was a nickname. His real name was too long for most people to remember.

"Efran, the boss wants me here now to look after things. He's tightening down the security. No leaks, understand."

"Of course, Eddy. We haven't had any leaks."

"We need to keep it that way. So, I'll be keeping an eye on you and your team."

"Please, stay away from the scientists. We need to keep them focused."

"Don't worry, the boss isn't concerned with them unless they try to escape." He grinned, turned, and walked away.

"Damn," Efran muttered to himself. He knew he couldn't stop Eddy from doing whatever he wanted to do. The guy stood over six feet tall and weighed over two hundred pounds. Not a giant, but he didn't lack in size. Besides, any disadvantage he might have against a larger opponent, he made up for in brute strength and sheer viciousness. He had no soul. Another demon, Efran thought.

Efran had never worked around Eddy. He had only met him on occasion at some celebrations Sonder had thrown in the past. He didn't know why Sonder thought he needed Eddy here. If he could work up the courage, he would ask Sonder the next time he saw him. Efran entered his own office and immediately took a gulp of ouzo directly from the bottle he kept in his desk drawer.

Chapter 25

Early Sunday morning, Clint stood in front of the hotel and watched Cher drive off in the taxi. He had insisted on paying for the taxi. His Saturday had been fun. More fun than he had expected. Cher had a great sense of humor. They visited some of the usual sites that Clint had already seen, but spent most of the day picnicking at the zoo and relaxing on the beach. After dark, they ended up back in Clint's room.

"No strings. You understand? No strings," Cher had said when they entered the hotel the night before.

"I understand, but can we still be friends?" Clint said, trying to hold back a grin.

She hit his arm, laughing, "Maybe."

Cher had been a passionate lover.

The taxi disappeared around a corner a couple blocks down the road, and Clint went back inside the hotel. The breakfast buffet had not yet opened, but there was fresh coffee in the adjacent bar room.

Clint sat down in the corner of the room. He checked his phone and, as expected, saw no messages. Cher had made an impact on him. Nothing major, Clint knew, he wasn't built that way. The dilemma that faced him now was more of a curiosity than anything else.

He had wanted to come to Greece for a couple of years to see Elina Eugeny. Ever since their crossing paths in Las Vegas, he had wanted to come to Athens to see her. This mission had given him a good chance to do that. He knew he would have to wait for the mission to end, but he was here.

He had not had any contact with Elina since Las Vegas, but he had still wanted to see her again under more normal circumstances. Now, he wondered if he would simply like to spend a few extra days with Cher. A minor dilemma, but it bothered him more than any worries he had of facing another terrorist.

"Day dreaming? You must have had a good night."

Clint looked up and saw Tish standing there. She had a croissant on a small plate that she placed on the table in front of him.

"Good morning," he said and looked over to the still closed buffet line.

"My back door access again."

"Well, thank you."

"I saw you earlier," she said. She left her comment hanging.

"I met her when I first arrived. She works at her family's restaurant not far from here."

"None of my business, but I'm glad you don't have to be all alone here in our fine city," Tish said.

"She's a nice lady. Took me to the zoo."

"The zoo," Tish laughed, "I haven't been there in years. What a great idea."

"If you don't mind my asking, is Tish a nickname?"

"A nickname?" she said, more to herself than to Clint. "Oh, yes, my name is Patricia. I grew up with everyone calling me Trish, but I changed it to Tish when I left home."

"I like it. I have another question for you."

"As easy as the first?"

"Maybe. Are you familiar with the Eugeny family?"

"Of course, everyone knows them. A very rich and powerful family."

"What can you tell me about Elina? I met her once," Clint said.

"You'll have better luck with your lady friend here," she motioned to the front entrance to the hotel.

"Just wondering, daydreaming as you said."

"She married a few months ago into another rich family. Her husband is a member of the Greek delegation to the UN. One of the top diplomats. They live in New York now. It was a big wedding in all the news."

"Oh." Clint said. He wasn't sure if he was disappointed or relieved.

Tish sat down in a chair next to him. "I hope she's not the reason you came to Athens." Her voice carried a hint of sympathy.

"No, but seeing her again was something I thought I might do while I was here."

"She's become a very powerful woman. Very wealthy. Smarter than her brothers, but we women usually are," she laughed.

"How's the old man doing?"

"You came all the way here with hopes of seeing her but didn't do any homework?"

"Guilty."

"Romantic," Tish shook her head. "Her father is still healthy and running half the businesses in Greece. I tell you what, I think you should introduce me to her father. In exchange for all the croissants, you know."

"I thought he's married."

"It doesn't matter here in Greece." She smiled again, and Clint knew she wasn't being serious.

"Now you're daydreaming."

"A girl should never get too old to dream, right?"

"Yes, that's right."

"I tell you what, let me get you a good breakfast. What would you like?"

Clint started to say not to bother, but gave in to a grumbling stomach.

Chapter 26

"Jack seemed quite nervous, didn't he?" Maurice said.

"Yes, he did. He may be under pressure, too," Melody said.

"Think if we don't get it right, and the mission, whatever it is, fails, he'll be in trouble?" Maurice asked.

"Could be, but it seemed to me something just happened," Melody said.

"I don't care what happens to him. He has not done anything personally, but he's on the team with the murderer," Hideki said.

Kim nodded but didn't say anything.

"Maybe they're close to executing whatever plan they have, and failure is not an option for Jack. It's crazy though, since we have been left pretty much in the dark," Maurice said.

"If they succeed in this mission, do you think they will get rid of us then, or will they keep us for some future project? I'm a little nervous over getting to the endgame," Kim said.

"Don't you feel bad about our helping them?" Hideki asked.

"Of course, we all do, but you saw what they did to Dean, and what they almost did to you," Melody said, answering for her.

"I know, I know, but I never thought I would allow myself to be used to murder other people. I feel bad. I also feel like I'm a coward."

"You're not, Hideki," Melody said.

Maurice wondered if Hideki was right, and they were all cowards. It wasn't a good feeling.

Kim stood up, took a few steps away from the table and then turned around, facing the other three. "This is not a new argument, nor is it worth pursuing. Only the person who orders the killing, and the person who pulls the trigger are guilty. Even a doctor who heals a murderer is enabling him to go out and kill again. The mechanic who fixes the killer's car that he then uses to go out to find his next victim is an enabler. It is right to feel bad about what we are doing. However, we either do it, or we tell them no and get ourselves killed. We could then feel righteous about ourselves while we are dying."

"She is right. We are only helping them improve a weapon that already exists, and maybe avoid detection. I don't like what we are doing, but I do not accept any guilt for their actions," Melody said.

"I know, but it still bothers me," Hideki said.

It bothered Maurice, too. After the guards escorted him back to his room, his worry turned into depression. Would he ever see his family again? He forced himself to think about his three fellow prisoners. They faced the same dilemma.

He had grown to like and respect them. He considered Hideki a genius, but he couldn't think of Hideki without believing he would witness his murder soon. Hideki was thin and the shortest in the group, and Maurice thought the stress of captivity had caused him to become a little thinner and paler.

Both Melody and Kim were good looking women. They both seemed fit to him, and both exuded self-confidence. He thought the two women and he would be considered top level scientists, a step below the rare genius level he would put Hideki.

He liked that Melody led the team. She didn't let others intimidate her. Even here, while she may be terrified inside, she remained level-headed and focused. Plus, she had gone through something terrible and had come out of it seemingly as strong, unbroken. He didn't know if he could.

Kim, although new, had impressed him, too. Thinking of her, he caught himself classifying her as the prettier of the two.

"What a stupid thought," he said out loud to the empty room. Here they all were prisoners about to die, and he starts thinking about how pretty one of his fellow prisoners was. One's looks don't mean anything here, he told himself, so get that out of your head.

He sat down on his bed and leaned against the wall. His mind drifted to freedom, his family, and then a thought that if they all survived, a possible reunion someday. Keep thinking good thoughts he told himself.

Chapter 27

Clint placed his gym bag he used as a carryon and his suitcase on the luggage rack in the first-class train cabin. The small room gave him privacy and some measure of comfort. It would take a while before the train would reach Thessaloniki, Greece.

He had retrieved the 9mm Beretta and two clips of ammunition from the train locker where Buzz said it would be. How the weapon showed up in the locker, or the one earlier in the locker in Innsbruck, was a mystery to him. He knew Deer could arrange flights on military aircraft. She held a high enough civilian rank in the government to allow her to request those, but that was child's play compared to getting weapons into overseas train lockers. Once, he had been hand delivered a pistol off a fishing boat.

Deer had no field staff to do it and going to another agency for support was out of the question. Section's absolute secrecy prevented any other agency from knowing about the hunters' existence. He would have to ask Buzz about it again. Last time, Buzz had ignored the question.

Yesterday's call from Deer had surprised him.

"Things are moving fast. I need you to get up to Thessaloniki. We've made reservations for you to be on the morning train. It's their express, but that only means it stops fewer times in between."

"What happened?" Clint had asked.

"The police raided the address you gave me. They found a

roomful of black-market cigarettes. A lucky break for us, our tip to them said drugs. They seized the computers. Interestingly, all three were expensive, sophisticated ones. The type you wouldn't expect at a black-marketers place of work."

"Did they get anything off them?"

"Not yet, but I didn't expect they would. I've had Dolly scrutinizing phone traffic, and we got a hit. We may get more when we better identify the computers, but that may be another day or so."

"You think the scientists are in Thessaloniki?"

"Don't know, but it may be one leg of the journey closer. What I do know is the raid resulted in a flurry of short cell phone calls from that section of Athens to Thessaloniki. Could be an interesting coincidence, but I want us to pursue it. The phones used were all burner phones."

Deer hadn't told him much more. Clint hadn't pressed her for more either. He knew they would tell him what he needed to know, and he figured Buzz would be calling him before he arrived at his destination.

A porter knocked on his door and offered to bring Clint a light lunch. He accepted, and a few minutes later the porter returned with a salami sandwich on a hard roll and a bottle of Mythos. He had come to like this Greek beer and wondered if he could buy this back in the States.

Clint watched the Greek countryside roll by outside while he munched on the sandwich. He knew a lot of the history he grew up being taught at school came from this part of the world. This region of Europe had been ruled by many masters, and for a few centuries the people from here ruled over their own large empire.

He leaned back, stretching over the couch and closed his eyes. His intuition and experience told him to rest now while he could.

The train came to a stop in the city of Velos, waking Clint up. A light rain fell and the room felt chillier than before. His phone vibrated on the small table next to his empty beer bottle. Right on time, he thought, smiling to himself.

"How's it going?" Buzz asked.

"Peaceful," Clint said.

"Good. Somebody just torched the address Deer had you check out in Athens. Not sure what they wanted to protect since the police had already seized everything."

"Does that mean we're on the right track?"

"Who knows? It means something, but what and to whom? Still, it's one of those coincidences no one believes in anymore."

Clint nodded in agreement. "What are the police saying?"

"The Athens police are wondering why the tip they received was wrong. No drugs, but the seizure of cigarettes appears to be more significant to them. It seems they'll get some sort of cut of the sales tax revenue the seizure will result in."

"Can't be much."

"No, but it may pay for a police picnic or something," Buzz said.

"Who owned the house?"

"Some very old woman. We don't know much about her yet, but it doesn't look like she had any role in this. She lives by herself ninety miles north of Athens."

"We booked you into a hotel near where the cruise ships come in. It's not too far from the train station. I don't know much about the city, but the region lays claim to Alexander the Great. You know he was Macedonian."

"You should have the boss send you here."

"I wish, but the way she's acting, I think we're getting close to the end game. She's had her head in the computers or on the phone all night. I had to bring her breakfast into her this morning. She's been here all night."

Clint remembered the time difference. He looked out the window and noticed the rain had started again. "I hope we're getting closer to the end game. It's raining outside, and the train is winding through some rugged countryside. I feel like I'm getting close to Transylvania."

"Dracula's home? Let's hope not. Although you're correct, that's actually not far from where you are right now."

"Great."

"I'll text you what you need to know before you arrive," Buzz said and the call ended.

The call didn't give Clint much more information than he already had, but it broke up the monotony of travel. He stood and stretched. The rain had turned into a mist and a light fog had developed. He wondered how far he was from Transylvania.

The trip was scheduled to take only four and a half hours but some issue with tracks turned the journey into a six hour one.

Chapter 28

Efran entered Sonder's office with more than a little trepidation. The text he received simply said, "My office, now!"

A step inside the office, Efran froze. Eddy was standing next to a man seated in front of Sonder's large desk. The man looked familiar, and despite his smile, the man looked terrified. In the corner two more men stood. They leaned against the wall and looked relaxed. More of Sonder's enforcers, Efran had seen them before, but he doubted he ever knew their names.

"Sit down," Sonder instructed, pointing to the other chair in front of his desk. Confused and even more frightened Efran did as he was told.

"I want you to pay attention and learn something," Sonder said to Efran.

"Yes, sir," Efran said. He had to force the words out his mouth.

"Do you know him?" Sonder asked and turned his head just enough to stare at the man sitting next to Efran.

Efran glanced over at the man. "No, sir."

Sonder nodded. "This man had the responsibility to keep some property of mine safe. A simple task, I thought. Keep it out of everyone's attention and protect it against all those thieves down in Athens."

"I didn't know---" the man started to say, but Eddy rapped the side of the man's head with his left hand.

"Shut up. You were supposed to keep the place clean. The

police wouldn't have done anything if it was clean. Why were all those cigarettes there?"

Efran could see the man wanted to respond, but Sonder's stare kept him silent.

"Almost a thousand cartons of cigarettes," Sonder tried to make his voice sound incredulous, but the venom in it made it sound more like a threat.

"Efran, one of two things happened here. Either he was involved in the use of my house for storing black-market cigarettes, or he had lost control of his men. You understand I can't tolerate either."

Efran nodded.

"Well, I burned down the house. More of an anger thing, the cops had already taken my computers. Some people think I have anger issues. Do I?"

"No, sir," the sweat started forming on Efran's forehead.

"Ha!" Sonder laughed. "Good for you, Jack."

Efran flinched. The way he called him Jack only increased his anxiety.

"So, how should I deal with this?"

"I don't know?"

"What was that, Jack? You said I shouldn't put up with it. Well, Eddy, if Efran thinks we shouldn't tolerate this behavior, maybe we should teach him a few manners."

Efran didn't notice if Sonder gave Eddy a signal, but out of the corner of his eye, he saw a blur to his right. He heard a loud crunching noise and a sound like someone gagging. Instinctively, he turned his head in time to see Eddy smash his fist into the man's face again. The man started to slump in his chair. Eddy took a second to line up and hit the man a third time in the face.

The man made no sound as he crumbled out of the chair and onto the floor. The man's face stared away from Efran, but what he could see seemed misshapen and bloody. More blood began to spread around his head.

"Clean him up and get him out of here," Sonder said.

The two men, who had been standing in the corner, dragged the man out if the room. The man tried to say something but Efran couldn't understand him.

"Eddy, go with them. Take him out on the boat and get rid of him. I don't want his body to be found."

Eddy grunted some reply, but Efran's eyes focused on the black glove Eddy was removing from his right hand. The glove appeared to be made out of leather and had several silver metal inlays that protruded from the glove like tiny pyramids. Something stuck to the glove fell off as the glove came off Eddy's hand. Efran watched it fall to the floor with the realization that it was likely a very small part of the poor man's face.

"His mistakes may affect our project. We are too close to allow anything to stop it. I will be cleaning up any trail to us, but someone is getting close."

"But how? Who?" Efran knew his voice sounded like that of a terrified child.

"I don't know, but somehow, they got to two of my best soldiers. Now my communications center in Athens has been compromised. By tomorrow evening, I want you to gather all the latest the scientists can give us. We'll have to settle for that."

"Yes, sir. Then what do you want to do with the scientists?"

"Nothing for a few days. We can decide later. Our client has expressed an interest in hitting only two targets. If we are successful, he will likely use us again, but for now our commitment is only these two. You will be a rich man, Efran. Of course, if you mess up, you could end up like your friend today." Sonder's stare made Efran look down at the desk.

"I won't."

"Go. Go play with your friends."

Efran left the room. In the elevator, he took a minute to steady himself. His hands shook, and he had to wipe away the sweat that ran down his face. His eyes had watered up, but thankfully he hadn't started crying. He entered the lab without any thought of what he would say. The four scientists stood huddled around their work table. He took a few steps toward them and stopped. They turned and looked at him.

"We will be working late today. We need to work hard." He stopped talking, not knowing what he should say next. Better to go back to his own office and get his thoughts organized. He turned around and left.

"What was that all about?" Maurice asked.

"No idea," Melody said.

"Was that blood on his pants' leg?" Hideki asked.

Chapter 29

Clint watched a cruise ship maneuver out of the harbor. The fourth-floor room at the hotel gave him an unobstructed view of the cruise ship and a large seagoing ferry, the two largest ships in the harbor. Dozens of other medium and smaller sized ships and boats lined the handful of docks visible from his room. One Greek naval or coast guard ship sat off shore in the distance.

His phone vibrated in his pocket.

"She wants you to walk by an industrial area about two miles from where you are. You should be able to follow the coastline to it, but I don't know if you have any beach there or not."

Clint hadn't seen a beach out his window.

Buzz continued, "There's a manufacturing facility there that specializes in remote controlled toys, to include drones. It's also the location where a number of phone calls were received after the police raid on the house in Athens."

"Sounds too good to be true," Clint said.

"It may be, but a place where you manufacture recreational drones would be a perfect cover to manufacture some lethal ones. She's trying to figure out how to get the Greeks interested in checking it out without any trace back to us. Being an industrial complex with a lot of different buildings and even other companies there, it's a little complicated."

"Has there been any interest in the place in the past by any other agency?"

"Unfortunately, no. Interpol and the FBI have identified a Sonder Agape as having financial dealings with the drone manufacturer. He lives in Thessaloniki and has financial fingers into half the things that go on in the region. Most of them illegitimate."

"A bad guy?"

"One of the worst, but we have nothing linking him to the scientists or anything outside of Greece. We checked him out during the Eugeny matter a couple of years ago, but other than verifying that he is a ruthless thug and among the top in the crime world in Greece, we decided he wasn't involved."

After the call, Clint decided to check the area out right away. He had a couple hours of daylight left, and a two-mile hike should only take him about forty-five minutes. He didn't mind being out after dark, but wandering around an industrial area after dark was never a good idea.

The young man at reception told him a sidewalk stretched along the water's edge for a long way in the direction he wanted to go. He offered Clint a couple of different city maps and even suggested a restaurant for dinner. He spoke very good English and told Clint he wanted to visit America. Clint had to finally excuse himself, or the young man might never have stopped talking.

Heavy clouds filled the sky, but the rain he had passed through while Clint was on the train had not arrived here. Clint hoped it would stay away. He found the paved walking trail along the sea and increased his pace to a fast walk. After ten minutes or so, he came upon a museum, a tall round building, and then a city block sized open area. His trail led directly to a large square paved in what looked like marble. A huge statue of Alexander the Great riding a horse stood in the middle of the square. A number of tourists mingled around it, and several school kids ran around, playing on the large grassy area adjacent to the square.

Clint continued his hike. The city buildings once again encroached on the trail, but with the sea to his right, the sense of being out in the open remained. A few joggers ran by him. He saw the large industrial area about the same time the paved path came to an end. He had to take an alley out to the first street to continue on his trek. A number of noisy bars and a few cafes dominated these last three city blocks before he came to a fork in the road. Turning left one skirted the back of a number of buildings before joining the city as it reformed around the street. The right fork led you through about a hundred yards of open land that reminded him of a "no-man's zone" before you would get to the series of warehouses and other industrial looking buildings. He started walking toward the buildings.

Cars approached him from the industrial district. Rush hour, he wondered as he watched a series of cars go by. Only a few passed him the other way, going into the large complex. He saw about a half dozen men and women walking toward him but on the other side of the road. Well-worn dirt paths paralleled both sides of the road.

He imagined people were going home from work, and the few cars heading into the complex were part of a shift change or possibly driving in to pick up someone. Either way, he didn't think his walk into the area would raise too many eyebrows. He only intended to stay a few minutes to get a feel for the place. He wasn't going to make any great discovery, nor had he been tasked to do more than take a quick look around.

The road bent to the left after it passed the first row of buildings. From there, Clint counted five roads all connecting to it from the right side. They each ran deeper into the complex, and Clint imagined other interior roads connected them.

He turned around when he reached the second side road. He had seen enough, and he had noticed more than one person staring at him. When he reached the point where the road veered right and headed back into the city, he noticed a well-worn path that led straight ahead to the large rocks that lined the shore. Clint took the path, thinking that's what a tourist would likely do.

Reaching the rocks, he saw the path continue to his left for about fifty yards to a spot behind a second building where two picnic tables had been placed. The shoreline appeared to curl inward just beyond the tables. Curiosity, as much as anything else, prompted Clint to walk to the tables where he sat down. He looked out over the water. The shoreline extended all the way back to the one remaining cruise ship in the distance. Although part of the sun still peeked out over the mountains to the west, some of the city lights had come on. This would be a nice place to take a break or eat your lunch he thought. He noticed dozens of cigarette butts on the ground but no other trash.

Although the path ended at the tables, he only had to walk another ten yards to see down the shoreline as it skirted past the back of the industrial complex. He observed two small docks positioned behind these buildings. He had seen enough and started to retrace his steps.

As Clint walked past the tables, two men walked out of the alley that ran between the two buildings and gave the workers easy access to the picnic area. They stopped and looked at him curiously as he walked by. Clint smiled and nodded and kept walking.

One of them shouted something at him in Greek.

Clint turned his head but kept walking. "I don't speak Greek. I'm a tourist."

The two men looked at each other. Clint turned his head back in the direction he was walking and continued. After a few steps, one of the men shouted in English, "Stop."

Clint glanced once again back at the men but kept walking. One of the two had his phone up to his head. The two didn't look like they were part of any security company. They both wore dark pants. One wore a grey, dirty sweatshirt, and the other had on a navy blue, pullover sweater that had seen better days. They looked in their early twenties. They started following him.

"Damn, I don't need this," Clint said to himself.

About ten yards before he would have cleared the building to his right, another young man came around the corner in front of him. He looked straight at Clint and started walking toward him, pulling a knife out of his pocket. This one looked a lot more serious than the first two.

"My boss doesn't like people sneaking behind his buildings," he said in English and stopped.

Clint also stopped. "I wasn't sneaking."

"You come with us. My boss needs to talk to you."

"No, I'm a tourist. I'm going back to my hotel."

The man took two quick steps toward Clint, raising his knife towards Clint's face.

Clint thought he might have only wanted to scare him, but

pointing a knife this close at his face was unacceptable. He grabbed the man's wrist and twisted. At the same time, he slammed the palm of his left hand into the man's elbow. The man grunted in pain and dropped the knife. Clint stepped forward and with both hands pushed the man hard in the chest. The man fell backwards.

Clint saw movement to his right and reacted in time to grab this second assailant as he rushed into him. Clint used the man's momentum to spin and throw the man down the slope and into the rocks. The third man had approached but showed hesitation. He still held his phone in his hand. Clint punched the man in his solar plexus and grabbed the phone out of his hand as the man fell to the ground. He threw the phone out toward the sea.

All three were incapacitated, but he knew they would be fine. The man in the rocks had already tried to stand but sat down and now held onto his ankle. Clint picked up the knife and tossed it out into the sea.

He knew he needed to leave the area without any further delay. The one hundred yard walk back to the semi-security of the city would take too long if someone came after him in a car. Running would bring too much attention to him. Fortunately, a city bus pulled to a stop across the street and a mere twenty-five yards away from him. A line of workers started to get on the bus. Clint hustled to reach the back of the line as the last person got on.

From the driver's reaction he must have over paid the fare. A man in work overalls two rows back from the front said, "You have given him too much money."

"That is the smallest I have. Tell him he can keep the extra for a coffee later."

He did, and the driver grunted and said something back to the man, causing a number of the passengers in the front rows to laugh.

"Please sit," the man translating for Clint said and gestured with his hand to the open seat across the aisle from him. "The driver said 'Screw the coffee, I need tsipouro after driving this bus all day'."

"I hadn't intended on taking a bus today. I was sightseeing along the sea, and when I got to this end of walk way, I thought I would walk down here before turning back. When I saw the bus, I decided I had walked enough."

The man nodded and smiled but didn't say anything more.

The bus turned to the right at the fork in the road, so Clint got off at the first stop. He didn't know the bus's destination, but he figured he could follow the route the bus had taken back the half mile or so it had driven. He hadn't walked far when he saw the sea down a side road. He took this shortcut toward the sea, knowing he could follow the coastline back to the hotel.

Instead of going all the way to the water, Clint turned onto a sidewalk beside a busy street that looked like it was the last road that ran alongside the sea. He passed numerous restaurants, shops, and professional offices on both sides of the street before arriving at a spot where he could see across the street to the grassy park and the statue of Alexander mounted on his horse. Children still played on the lawn and tourists still surrounded the statue in the semi-darkness of the early evening.

Chapter 30

"What do you mean the three of you couldn't handle one man?" Sonder snarled at the three wounded and bruised young men standing in front of him.

"He was no amateur," the leader of the three said. He held his right elbow with his left hand, keeping it immobile and close to his body.

"You said he wasn't Greek?"

"Yes, sir. At first I thought he was, but he said he wasn't. I think he was an American."

"Do you even speak enough English to understand what he said?"

"I speak a little, but he understood. He said he wouldn't come with us when I told him my boss wanted to speak to him."

"Who the hell were you going to take him to?" Sonder's tone made it a question none of the three felt safe to answer.

"I'm not sure. It's just what I said. No one else has ever defied us before." The young man's eyes stared down at his damaged elbow.

"That's because the others were Greeks who were all too happy to tell you who they were to stay out of trouble. If you see this man again, don't bother him, but come tell me or Eddy immediately. You understand?"

"Yes, sir," all three answered. They started to leave.

"One more thing," Sonder interrupted their departure. "If you have to take someone to your boss in the future, take them to the security office, not here to this building or to me."

After the three left, Sonder summoned his receptionist.

She came in with a cold unopened beer and brought it to him. He took the beer with one hand and her arm with the other. He pulled her onto his lap. She didn't resist. She knew what all this job entailed long before she convinced Sonder to hire her. She considered him a distasteful, sadistic brute, but she had grown up with too many men and women like that in her life to let those qualities affect her. She liked the perks that came with the job: the money, the status, the relative safety. No one messed with her now. Her two main responsibilities took little to no effort. She had to maintain absolute secrecy about everything that Sonder said or did. Second, she had to be compliant. In her case, she had honed both these skills by the time she was a young teenager.

"Has anyone been asking any questions about what we're doing?" Sonder asked. He smiled, but she didn't see any happiness in that smile.

"No, nobody asks me any question. They know I know nothing. I just answer phone calls and relay messages."

"Have you received any strange phone calls recently?"

"No, sir," she began to get frightened.

"You know, the woman you replaced now has an easy job at my resort in Jamaica. The one before her at my house in Scotland. They both were very loyal to me. Have I ever told you what happened to the one before her?"

She shook her head. Sonder saw tears begin to form.

"I gave her to Eddy and the boys to have fun with before they slowly fed her to the pigs on my farm. She talked too much."

The tear began to run down her face. "I swear."

"Okay, I do believe you, but I have a leak somewhere. Don't let me find out it was you. You can go."

"Yes, sir. Can I do anything for you to help you relax before I go?"

"No, not today. I've got to take care of a few things, but keep asking, and tell Efran I need to see him."

She hurried out of Sonder's office.

Efran arrived at his office a few minutes later. It had been a couple days since he had last sat in the chair in front of Sonder. The fear he had felt then returned.

"We may have a problem. Do you trust everyone on your team?"

"My team? You mean the four who support me and work with the scientists?"

"Do you have another team?" Sonder asked in a louder voice.

"No, no sir, I just didn't understand. Yes, I trust them. They don't fully understand what we are doing, and none of them have asked for any real explanation. They believe we are trying to build a sophisticated set of drones to sell. They don't know any more, and they know the effort is secret. They might think we are building the drones for our military. At least, I haven't discouraged that idea."

Sonder leaned back in his chair and thought about that. "Good, good, let them continue to think that, but remind them to keep their mouths shut."

"I will. May I ask what has happened?" Efran hoped he wasn't pushing his luck.

"An American was snooping around out back. The fools I

have to keep people from doing that got their asses whipped by him. I was thinking that the raid in Athens on my house was a local police matter, but now I'm beginning to wonder. Tomorrow we will fulfill our contract. If it is successful, we may not need to keep your friends anymore."

"Won't our client want to continue with our service?"

"Maybe, but there are always other clients. If it all goes well, I was thinking of releasing your friends. We would have to take them somewhere before we did and, of course, threaten their families if they talked. You may go," Sonder said.

He watched as Efran left the office. He grinned, knowing he already lined up a buyer for the two women. He had no intention to let the two male scientists leave alive.

Efran returned to his own office wondering why Sonder had said he might let the scientists live. He knew Sonder would never release them. Did Sonder think he needed to tell him that to keep him from doing something crazy these next few days? If so, it meant Sonder had his concerns about him, and that was no good.

Efran did not believe any of his team would compromise what they were doing. Besides, as he had mentioned to Sonder, they really didn't know. For that matter, he didn't know the target either.

Chapter 31

"Our situation aside, we work pretty good together," Melody said.

Hideki grinned. "You three have kept me from going crazy. If we get out of here alive, maybe we should form some type of business partnership."

Maurice felt like saying there was little chance of them being set free, but kept quiet. It felt good to dream a little.

"I think whatever our captors have been up to is close to happening. I have mixed feelings about it. If it succeeds, they may want to keep us longer and do more. If it fails, they will likely punish us," Maurice said.

"Unfortunately, I find myself hoping it succeeds. Isn't that terrible," Hideki said more as a statement than a question.

"Let's get back to happy thoughts, Hideki. What kind of partnership would we be, and what would be its purpose?" Melody asked.

"A consulting partnership."

"Equal partners?" Kim asked, raising her eyebrows.

"Absolutely."

"Hideki, your idea is a good one. I have a friend who can write up all the legalese to make it happen. He owes me," Maurice said.

"It's a deal, then," Melody said and put her fist out over the table.

The other three did the same, and they all bumped fists.

"I have a thought, what if we completely redesigned the

drone's structure? It's a thought I've had for some time," Kim said.

"Explain, please, we have nothing better to do today. Jack took our latest yesterday and didn't give us any new instructions. This could be our first step as a new partnership," Melody said.

Maurice nodded his head, but Jack had always given them new instructions. The fact that he hadn't increased Maurice's anxiety. He couldn't shake the feeling that something terrible was about to happen to all of them.

Over the next three hours the scientists immersed themselves into a hypothetical discussion about a totally new design for a small drone. Maurice enjoyed the activity, something he referred to as creative brainstorming.

Jack interrupted them when he entered the lab with the usual guards.

"Time to return to your rooms. We will be testing your efforts today. Let's all hope for success. Tomorrow we will have new instructions for you."

Like obedient pets, the four stood up and went with their guards to their rooms.

"Remember, we're partners," Melody said as the group separated.

A horrible dread encompassed Maurice, and he felt like he was suffocating. It let up a little when the guard closed the door to his room, leaving Maurice, once again, alone.

Melody must have felt like he did. That's why she said what she had. If nothing else, they would suffer the same fate. He admired her. If they did survive this and were able to form a partnership, he would always consider her as the leader.

Without her grit and backbone, he doubted whether he or Hideki could have held up under the stress.

Kim's mind impressed him. She, like Hideki, was brilliant, but while she pretended to put up a brave front, he could see the fear that was in her eyes whenever Jack came into the lab. Jack was one of the bad guys, but compared to his boss he was nothing. Maurice had the impression that Jack really wanted the four of them to succeed in their tasks. Not just for him, but also to keep away whatever evil lay outside the lab.

Maurice thought about Jack for a while, wondering how he got mixed up with this. A guard came and brought his dinner. The meal consisted of a small bowl of what looked like goulash soup. He wondered if prisoners in real jails were fed better.

After his dinner, Maurice sat back on his bed and leaned against the wall. As he did every night, he tried to dream of his family. He had already made a mental list of twenty vacations he would take with his family once he was free.

Deep into a dream, Maurice didn't register what he was hearing at first. Why was someone in his dream screaming? In a sudden jerk, Maurice came back to reality and strained to hear what was happening outside his room. The screaming had stopped, but after a short silence, he could hear a woman crying or pleading. It only lasted for a few seconds, then everything became silent again.

It had to be Kim. They had talked, and they had agreed he had heard her the first couple of nights after she had arrived. No one else had heard her. What had they done to her? Were they starting the process of killing them off? He hoped not. Maybe they were just having some fun at her expense. He hoped that was all.

Then, he hated himself for hoping for that.

No one came for him in the morning. He knew it was an irrational thought, but he knew that when someone finally came for him, it would be to kill him or take him somewhere to be killed. He didn't get dressed. No breakfast came. No lunch came.

He sat on his bed and prayed. He willed thoughts of his love for his family. Like telepathic messages, he concentrated with all his effort to send these messages to his family. One to each, like a dying man might write to his loved ones.

The door finally opened. A big man, as ugly as he was terrifying, stood there grinning at him.

Chapter 32

A black limousine, gleaming in the bright African sun, pulled up in front of a half dozen similar vehicles. An individual jumped out of the front passenger seat and opened the back passenger door. This man had a large revolver, holstered, but on display for everyone to see. Another man wearing a flowered, Hawaiian-style shirt climbed out of the back seat.

The man in the flowered shirt looked up at the large house. Three guards armed with what might have been military grade automatic rifles stood alert on the front porch that spanned the full length of the house. His host hustled down the steps to greet him.

"It is an honor —." An explosion interrupted the host's welcome.

Besides the shock of the noise, pieces of his guest blew into him at such force that fragments of bone pierced his skin and clothing in dozens of places. The force of the explosion knocked him back into a sitting position on one of the steps. Stunned, he was certain he saw the bottom half of his guest still standing in front of him for a full second before it dropped straight down.

Two of the guards from the porch raced down next to him; however, the host did not notice them or the guard dogs barking in the distance. He hadn't been severely wounded, but shock had set in, and it would be another twenty minutes before he became coherent.

****

The call came in while Clint was walking by a school yard. A hundred or so boys and girls were running around, playing, and making a lot of noise. He had walked to an area near the harbor where he watched a Viking cruise ship dock at the large pier.

"Give me a minute to get away from this noise," Clint said. He hurried across the street and kept walking away from the school. "Okay, this is better, what's up?"

"We think they've hit their primary target," Buzz said.

"You mean the drone people?"

"Yes."

"Several hours ago, well, late morning in Africa, a Moussef Polini, I'm sure I'm massacring his name, was killed by what we believe was a drone strike. We don't know all the details, and I'm not sure we will. It appears that a small projectile stuck Polini on his back and exploded on contact."

"Any witnesses?"

"Many. Guards and guests who were watching out the window at Polini's arrival. The statements they gave were similar to the statements of the Israeli athletes who survived the bus attack. Several of them saw something streak through the sky and strike Polini. They described it as a small blur. One guard said he shouted a warning but the object moved so fast by the time he shouted the thing struck Polini."

"Did it kill him right away?"

"Yes, it apparently ripped him apart.?"

The image of too many incidents in Southwest Asia ran through Clint's mind.

"Did they see where the rocket or drone came from?" Clint asked.

"Not really, but one person thought they saw something flying away in the distance after the explosion. At first, he thought it was a high-flying bird, but afterwards he wondered if it could have been something else."

"So, if we're assuming the scientists are somewhere around here, the people behind the drones must be doing this for some rich client in Africa."

"Exactly," Buzz said. "She already has an idea who, too."

"That should make things easier."

"Possibly a little. The person killed was extremely wealthy. He ran a company that was supposedly state regulated. The company controlled all the rights to a variety of rare, special metals that are mined there. He is or was little known outside Africa, but from all accounts he was a popular figure. He led a number of charities and supported a number of agricultural initiatives to help the small farmer."

"Sounds like he wasn't a bad guy."

"In the scheme of things, he probably wasn't. I would like to say especially in that part of the world, but we have too many like him here," Buzz said.

Clint didn't know which scheme of things Buzz referred to or which wealthy Americans he had in mind. He didn't care either.

"Why such an elaborate method to kill him?"

"The man lived in a fortress, was always surrounded by security, and traveled in an armored car. He was impossible to get close to without some serious vetting. The private residence where he was killed is itself a fortress. Guards, guard dogs, big metal fence, a hundred and fifty yards of cleared land between the house and the tree line. The fence was another fifty yards further out. Security cameras and lights scattered about."

"I see. Like your house."

"I wish. His host was a lifelong friend and another very wealthy man," Buzz said.

"What would be the motive?"

"For a hit like this, it has to be money or power. Likely both come hand-in-hand. Our prime suspect was also in the house at the time. There was going to be some big meeting of ten or so of the country's most powerful individuals to discuss future initiatives."

"It will be hard to pin the murder on someone who was in the house with the others," Clint said.

"We know, and at this point we just hope the event may end up giving us more leads. Deer is focused on the scientists and the drones."

"I guess it's too early to have anything already. You said you suspect someone else in the house. Why is that?"

"The victim had total control over exports worth billions of dollars a year. There is some semblance of state control, but according to the CIA, the victim had everyone in his pockets. The president, key staff, the nation's inspector general, you name it. But listen to this, the agency considered him one of the good guys in the region. He was apolitical and, as far as we know, not involved in any serious criminal enterprises."

"I guess when you have a billion dollars to play with you can do a lot of things without resorting to crime. Bribery excluded, of course," Clints said.

"He kept his workers, and there are thousands of them, content by paying his workers enough to keep them out of poverty. That and he sponsored a handful of international charities to come to his country three or four times a year and offer free medical clinics for his workers."

"What's in it for this suspect?"

"The two have been serious competitors for years. They're actually distant cousins. Our suspect has a grip on the alcohol and tobacco trade. Lucrative in its own right, but its revenue is only a quarter of the precious metals mining and trade that Polini had. Deer thinks he'll make a grab for it."

"Is this anything more than background for me?"

"No, that's all this is, but I find it all fascinating. In my free time, I'll spend my time analyzing it. It will make for a good study. Help us out with our cover."

"You'll have to tell me about it over a beer sometime. Anything for me now?"

"No, but Clint, Deer thinks this may end the need for the scientists by whoever has them. Things may happen fast. Keep your phone nearby."

The call ended. Clint thought about the call. His tours of duty with the military that took him throughout the Middle East and Southwest Asia taught him a lot about the relationship between the rich and the government. The large cities operated similar to the countries. The wealthiest citizens had significant control over the governments, because the government leaders made most their money from bribes and kickbacks from the rich.

Usually, the governments had limited resources to enforce the customs over imports and the taxation from the sale of goods. Corruption became the norm, and on occasion it worked well for the remainder of society.

Clint had already informed Section about his run in with

the three men at the industrial complex. They agreed he should stay away for the time being. The incident stoked his curiosity, so rather than do nothing, Clint rented a motorcycle and located a number of vantage points where he could park and watch the complex with binoculars.

He had done this for a couple of days, enjoying the sights of the city more than learning much from his surveillance efforts. However, he did find a few spots from where he could better observe the large buildings in the complex that backed to the sea and had their own docks. He explored the roads outside the city and found spots near the coastline where he could look back and see the city shoreline from a distance. On one occasion he saw a small boat tied up to the dock behind one of the buildings.

The sun had started its descent behind the mountains to the west when Deer called him. He was sitting on a section of the old rock wall that was part of the ancient city. The spot allowed him to overlook Thessaloniki and out to the sea. His binoculars did little good up here, but he liked the place. Unlike Athens and Madrid, he had not met anyone here with whom he could spend time, but this solitude helped him relax.

"We got our break, Clint. Within hours of the death of Polini, ten million dollars were transferred out of an account controlled by our suspect in Africa to an account controlled by a Sonder Agape. It went through two off shore accounts, but our financial surveillance capabilities are pretty impressive these days."

"You mentioned this Sonder guy before, right?"

"He lives right there where you are. He's a nasty guy and runs a criminal enterprise that would impress the Mafia of old.

More significant is the fact that he owns the recreational drone manufacturing plant right where those three thugs assaulted you."

"Bingo," Clint said, now remembering the earlier conversation.

"Yes. Buzz was able to get with a couple State Department analysts and his CIA friend to work up a threat study for the Community. He steered them to the money angle. Needless to say, everyone's excited."

"Do you want me to leave?"

"No. From all accounts the local and national police in the region may have some leaks. Maybe worse. Sonder is a slippery guy and has lots of contacts throughout the Macedonia region. He might try to disappear. If he breaks free, he's your target. I'll be sending you a few photos."

"What about the scientists?"

"It may be too late to help them, but we hope the Greeks will be looking for them. I imagine their home countries may make an effort now, too."

The call ended.

Chapter 33

Maurice stared at the man at the door.

"Come," Eddy grunted with a heavy accent.

"What? Where are we going?" He didn't see a weapon on the man, but Maurice knew that didn't matter.

The man didn't answer. He took five quick steps and grabbed Maurice by his face. The big man's hand clamped down and yanked Maurice toward him. He then pushed him by the head toward the chair where Maurice had tossed his clothes the night before.

Maurice dressed, and the man motioned him to move toward the door. Two armed guards stood outside the door. Maurice joined them. He noticed the two guards hurry out of the big guy's way and did not make eye contact with him. Maurice realized they were afraid of him, too.

The big man started walking, and one of the guards had to prod Maurice with his weapon to get him to move. Maurice had trouble making his legs move. Terrified, he thought he might get sick. The second, more vigorous poke of the gun barrel focused his mind enough that he began walking.

They walked to the end of the hall and followed the corner around to the left. Halfway down this hall, a third guard stood outside a door. He opened it, and the big man went into the room. Maurice couldn't see inside, but he heard Hideki let out a frightened squeal. A second later, the big man dragged Hideki out by the ankle and kicked him to make him stand up.

"Get up," the third guard said. His tone wasn't harsh. "Why

make it worse."

Maurice watched as Hideki looked at the guard and started to stand up. The big man grabbed Hideki by the arm and lifted him, pulling Hideki's face within inches of his own. Hideki visibly trembled but remained silent.

The big guy let go of Hideki, turned, and started walking away.

"Follow him," the guard said.

"What's happening?" Maurice asked.

Eddy stopped and looked back at the guard who had been talking. The guard said something in Greek.

Maurice could see this third guard, despite holding a weapon, was also frightened of the big man. He must be a monster, Maurice thought.

"Be quiet. He does not want us to talk. He doesn't understand English. Don't make it worse," the guard said. He moved away from them.

The four reached a stairwell and took the stairs up two flights to a door that opened to the darkness outside. Maurice saw the sea and smelled the fresh air. The false feeling of freedom only lasted a few seconds as they were led down a short pier to a boat. Once on the boat the guards forced them into a small storage compartment below the deck. A door was closed and locked behind them. Enough light came in through the gaps around the door and through a crack above the door to let them see around the room.

"They're going to kill us," Hideki said. His voice, laced with fear, sounded almost like a whimper.

"Stay calm. Our only chance is to stay calm." Maurice checked the door to ensure it was locked.

"I'm not a good swimmer," Hideki said.

"And have our bodies wash up on shore? They probably won't do that. We're next to a big city. Didn't you see the lights of the city when they put us on this boat?"

"Yes, but what city. And you don't know the currents. They may take us away from land."

Maurice knew Hideki's assumption that they would be killed and thrown overboard was likely correct, but he wanted to change Hideki's attitude.

"Hideki, we can't give up. We're smarter than these guys. We might not be able to overpower them, but—"

"There's no might not about it. That big guy could handle both of us by himself, and they have guns," Hideki said, interrupting Maurice.

"I know, but we can't just give up. We need to come up with a plan. Maybe more than one plan, since we don't know what to expect. Let's plan for different contingencies. I don't plan to die without a fight."

Hideki smiled at his friend. "You're a lot more optimistic than I am. It's a good trait. I like that in you. I'm more fatalistic, but let's do it your way. It may at least take my mind off drowning."

"Good."

"I've always thought the worst way to go is by drowning, by burning, or by being crushed," Hideki said.

"Hey! Stop that. When we get out of here, I'm going to find you a good therapist to keep you from always thinking about how you might die."

"Maybe one of your American red heads. They've always fascinated me," he smiled.

"A red head? Not a blond therapist?"

"Actually, it doesn't matter, I think I'm more attracted to their eyes."

"Among other things," Maurice said, and they both laughed.

"They haven't tied us up. Do you think that means they might let us go?"

"That's a big swing. A few seconds ago, you were sure they were going to kill us. I think if they were going to let us go, they would have said something. I don't think I would believe them, but if they were going to let us go, they wouldn't want us to do something stupid."

"Something else, I keep thinking. If they were going to let us go, I believe Jack would have been there when we were taken to the boat to reassure us. I know that's just my thinking, but he would want to reassure us and maybe plead with us to stay quiet. I don't think he is a violent man."

"I think you're right. Although he pushed us and definitely knew what was going on, he, personally, never threatened us," Maurice said.

"So, what's the plan?"

"I don't have one specific plan. I think we need to think of the various situations we may face, and how we should react to them."

"For example?"

"What if one of the guards got sloppy and set his rifle down. Should we try to grab it?"

"I wouldn't know how to operate it. I mean I could point and squeeze the trigger, but if I needed to do another step, I'd be lost," Hideki said.

"Me, too, but would it be worth the chance?"

"Only if death was imminent."

"I agree. How about jumping overboard. They haven't tied us up. It's dark outside, so we might be able to escape."

"Best case would be that one of us might get away. It would be too easy for the boat to follow one of us. If we could slip over the side of the boat without anyone noticing, we might have a head start. Although, like I said, I'm not a good swimmer."

"Okay, it's a long shot, but if the opportunity presents itself, we ought to try it," Maurice said.

"I doubt that we will get the opportunity. What if they leave us here and sink the boat with us on it?"

"I'm not sure we're worth sinking the boat, but if they did, they would likely leave the door locked."

"We could remove the hinges if we had a screwdriver, or we could simply pop out the rods holding the hinges together. What do we have in here we can use?"

Their eyes had adjusted to the dim light in the room. They both moved around the room looking for anything useful.

"This room doesn't look like it's been used for anything. The shelves are bare. There's nothing here," Hideki said.

"I hate to think they just use this place to transport their victims."

"It's good that it's too dark in here to look for blood stains. What's this?" Hideki bent over and picked up a thin nail. "Want it?"

"If you don't," Maurice said and extended his hand. "Not sure what use it might have, but I would even grasp at a straw if we found one." He studied the nail. "No, you found it, you hang onto it."

"I'm glad I'm not alone right now. You're a good man. Braver than me. Why didn't they bring Melody and Kim with us?"

"They mentioned they had different plans for them, didn't they. I hate to think what they meant." Maurice couldn't get himself to say they were going to sell them.

The boat engine cut way back to an idle.

"We're stopping," Hideki said, his voice pitched high again.

"It's only been twenty to thirty minutes. We can't have gone far or be too far off shore," Maurice said.

The boat continued to move, but they were definitely slowing down.

"Please, God," Maurice whispered.

Chapter 34

"Have a drink, Efran," Sonder said.

Efran accepted a small glass.

"It's an American whiskey. We celebrate a successful completion of our biggest job. More importantly, we just received our payment. Ten million Euros, Efran, that's what your team helped us achieve."

"Ten million, that is amazing, sir," Efran said. The amount did impress him, and he tried to show that in his expression. However, he couldn't shake the experience of the night before. It still repulsed him. As he had before with Melody, Sonder had forced him to watch as he brutalized and raped Kim. He had wanted Efran to do the same after he was finished with her, but he couldn't.

Sonder had laughed at him. "You are too soft. You will always be a sheep, Efran, but you are a good worker. We will be clearing out today. I think someone is closing in on us. Some outside agency, not Greek, but they may soon follow. I need the lab sanitized. Your assistants will each get a bonus and sent on holiday. Remind them to talk is to die a painful death."

"Of course, I will," Efran said.

"Do not worry about your four scientists. That is not your concern. You will get a nice bonus in a few days. Do I need to remind you what will happen if you cross me?"

"No," Efran took another sip of the whiskey. He hoped Sonder didn't see his hand shake.

"Good, because I would feel bad after our long association

if I sent Eddy to visit your wife. He's not as sensitive as I am."

Efran thought he might pass out. His head throbbed. "Please, I will never betray you. I promise."

"I know. The two men will be leaving us this evening and the two women just before dawn tomorrow. You do not need to be involved. How long before you can get rid of everything from the lab?"

"That should not take long. I have all the data on a thumb drive. The factory also has a copy. What should we do with those?"

"We keep them. We also have the drones. I shall have those kept somewhere. The section of the plant we set aside for our little secret project will be opened back up to the main factory. By this time tomorrow, all evidence of the manufacture of our killer drones will be gone from here," Sonder said.

"Would you mind if I took leave, too. I would like to take my wife to Venice. We have never been there."

"No, have a good time. I should take my wife there someday. You can go. Send my girl in and lock the outer office door behind you. I don't want to be interrupted."

Efran left with mixed feelings of elation and guilt. The prospect of taking his wife to Venice made him happy. He knew she would be ecstatic. The bonus would be nice, too. Yet, he knew Sonder would have his four scientists killed or worse for the women. The thought made him sad. He knew the sadness and guilt would linger for a while, but he could do nothing about it.

Efran called his assistants to the lab and the five men removed the computers and anything else that could compromise what had been done there. They used a strong cleaner on the desk and table tops. When they had finished, Efran had them all sit around the table.

"Our job here is over. Our boss is extremely happy with what we accomplished. You will each be receiving a nice bonus soon. With that the boss wants each of you to take a vacation. Take your families or just your wife or girlfriend, but get out of the area for a while. Understand?"

All four nodded, and one asked, "How long should we be gone?"

"A week maybe two. It doesn't really matter. Call me when you get back, and I will let you know. Don't worry, your salary will continue, and the leave will not count against you," Efran said.

"Sounds too good to be true," the same man said.

"It's a good deal, but remember, and I cannot stress this strong enough, you must not ever mention anything about what we've been doing in this lab or the presence of the scientists to anyone. Do not ask why," Efran said, looking at one of the men who had started to say something.

"You all know who we work for. While we are employed to develop and assist in the manufacture of drones, you all also know this project has been a little different. The boss does not want anyone to know what we've been doing. This is a warning, not a threat, but if the boss gets any idea that any of you have discussed what we've been doing with anyone outside this room, he will sic Eddy on you and your families."

At this comment, all four men reacted. Two sat back like they needed to distance themselves from what Efran had just said. One of the men started saying they wouldn't say anything, and the last man stared back at Efran.

"We do know who we work for," this fourth man said. "We tell ourselves that what he does is not our concern. We have legitimate jobs. Yet, we all know the four, no five scientists, didn't come here of their own free will. We know this job was different. We know what we have done can put us all in jail. So, beyond the fear of the boss, none of us want to go to jail either. We will remain quiet."

"Good. I enjoyed working with all of you. Go home," Efran said.

They left, and Efran did one last sweep of the room to ensure nothing was missed. He then returned to his office and checked it for any scraps of paper or extraneous thumb drives. He deleted all the emails, documents, and pictures from his office computer.

After today, he didn't plan on coming back to this office. He had his own office and work area in the small building behind his house.

The next morning, Efran discovered the bonus had already arrived in his bank account. Twenty-five thousand Euros, more than four months of his normal income had been deposited. He surprised his wife at lunch with the news of their trip to Venice. He had already made their reservations. They would be leaving the next morning and stay for at least a week, maybe longer. The news thrilled her. He couldn't remember seeing her so happy. As they packed that night, he thought they may never come back.

Chapter 35

Clint leaned back against the large boulder. He had finished his hard roll, ham and cheese sandwich when the last of the sunlight faded from the sky. The calm sea lapped up against the shore below him and barely fifteen yards away. He discovered this spot the day before. Besides offering a nice ocean view to anyone who might venture off the beaten path, this spot gave Clint an excellent location from which he could observe the back of the buildings in which Deer had an interest.

Through his binoculars, Clint could clearly see a man on a boat that had been tied up to one of the small piers behind the building. The man sat on the edge of the boat and appeared to be waiting for something. The moon was still low in the horizon with only a third of it reflecting sunlight. It wouldn't be much help tonight, Clint thought, but maybe that would be good.

The pier had its own light. In fact, four pole lights kept the back of the buildings lit up at night, with one being adjacent to the pier Clint now watched. Earlier in the day, Buzz had called him.

"Try to find a good vantage point to watch the building we've highlighted on the text we just sent you. We think that's the one Sonder Agape owns and where his company builds its drones. It's a legitimate business, and it would be the perfect place to manufacture the killer drones."

"What am I looking for?"

"Good question. We'll also be sending you photos of the

five missing scientists. Deer believes that whatever is going to happen to them will happen in the next forty-eight hours. It's a long shot, but she's convinced you're at the right spot. We've passed on our thoughts, and we know the Greek authorities have been informed. Unfortunately, we also know that the Greeks are hesitant to do anything without more specific evidence."

"That's understandable. You've got the advantage of being able to connect the dots. At this point. I imagine the Greeks don't even know where the dots are," Clint said.

"Agreed. What's worse is that we believe as you get closer to Thessaloniki, the authorities become less interested in going after Agape."

"If I see something?"

"Let us know."

"That's it?"

"At this point, yes," Buzz said, and the call ended.

Clint had thought about it and had decided to make a picnic of it. He considered bringing a bottle of wine, but he had brought the sandwich, some olives, and a bottle of water with him instead of the wine. If he had to sit out here all night, he thought he might as well make it pleasant. He didn't think he would see anything.

If they were going to kill the scientists, why move them first. Kill them in the building and load them in a van or truck and dump their bodies somewhere in the country. He would have no chance to know which van or truck leaving the complex would have the bodies in it.

His only chance to see something would be if they took the bodies out to the sea. He might be able to see them carrying the bodies out to the boat. Even if they bagged the bodies or body parts, moving five individuals in any shape to a boat would be hard to miss.

Dumping the bodies at sea would be risky as something may wash up on shore, but weights could keep them down and currents could move them away from shore. People who lived here who were used to dumping things in the sea may know where and how to do it.

At ten o'clock, Clint started wondering if he should've worn a heavier jacket. The black leather jacket he had on seemed more than enough protection when he left the hotel. Now, however, with the breeze coming off the water, the cold started to penetrate it. He put his black leather gloves on just as he noticed movement on the pier. Grabbing the binoculars, Clint surveilled the pier and the boat. A second man had come out and walked up to the boat. This man carried a rifle, maybe an AR-15.

Seconds later, the door to the building opened, and a group of people walked out. The two men dressed in all white immediately caught his attention. He adjusted the focus on the binoculars until he was sure of what he saw. While he couldn't be sure of the taller man in white, he was certain the second man was one of the scientists. He watched the two men in white as they were marched onto the boat and then down inside.

Clint counted three armed men and one big, rough looking man board the boat. The boat left the pier. The sound of its motor could not be heard in the distance.

"Bingo," Clint said to himself. He called Section.

"What's happening?" Deer asked. No hello, just the question.

"Two male scientists were just loaded onto a boat, maybe a thirty or forty-footer, by some armed men. The boat has left the pier and is heading out to sea. No, wait, it appears to be headed in my direction paralleling the coastline. It may be a quarter mile offshore."

"Just two men, and could you identify them?"

"Yes, only two. I'm certain one was Hideki, the Japanese scientist. The other I believe was the American, Hockenberry."

"Interesting, I wonder what happened to the third one," Deer said.

"And the two women."

"It wouldn't surprise me if they didn't have different plans for the women."

Clint didn't need an explanation.

"They will be passing right in front of me."

"Can you follow them? I'd be interested in where they are going."

"As long as they follow the coast, I can stay on the road that runs along the coast line. I'm not sure how far it goes."

"Stay with them for as long as you can, and be careful." She ended the call abruptly.

Clint drove the motorcycle he had rented onto the dirt trail the hundred yards to the road. Turning right on the paved road, he glanced over at the water, but too many trees blocked his view. He drove for almost a mile before he had a clear view of the sea again. He didn't see the boat, but he knew he had to be quite a distance in front of it. The road approached the water at this spot and for a forty-yard stretch had no obstruction blocking his view. However, a rock cliff to his right, some twenty to thirty feet high, blocked his view back to where he thought the boat might be.

He turned off the engine and listened. After a few seconds, the faint sound of a boat's motor drifted to him. Clint drove the motorcycle back to the where the trees lined the road and hid it behind them. Staying in the trees, he walked to, but not into, the open patch of land next to the water. He didn't think anyone on the boat would be watching the shoreline, but it made sense to stay hidden.

A car drove by the road heading away from Thessaloniki. A good sign, Clint thought. The road must go somewhere. Once the sound of the car dissipated, the noise from the boat became clearer. A few minutes later, it came into view. Besides its running lights, the boat had a light on near its stern. He scrutinized the boat through his binoculars. If it docked among other boats, Clint wanted to be able to pick it out.

Three armed men sat in the back of the boat. Everyone else must be inside. Clint believed the boat was too close to shore to toss anyone, dead or alive, overboard.

"Where are you going?" Clint said out loud.

He continued driving and once again lost sight of the sea. After another mile, Clint slowed down. He didn't want to get too far ahead of the boat. The road hadn't passed any houses or businesses. Looking ahead, Clint didn't see any sign of life. He started to speed up when he passed a one lane dirt road that ran off the road toward the sea.

Clint made a U-turn and steered the motorcycle down the dirt road. Weeds had taken over most of the road, leaving tire or wheel tracks but not much more. Three or four minutes of slow riding took him to a chain link gate. A pad lock secured the gate and a sign in Greek warned people to stay out. Clint couldn't read the Greek, but he recognized the picture of a snarling dog placed at the bottom of the warning.

He didn't see any sign of security cameras, so he looked through his binoculars to see what he could. The land had been cleared ahead of him, and he could make out half of a house. Trees that continued a good thirty yards inside the fence line blocked the view to the other half. More importantly, Clint saw the sea behind the house.

Clint hid the motorcycle in some bushes and started walking along the fence line. He figured the fence continued to or near the water. If this wasn't the boat's destination, he might at least watch it go by.

The fence did run all the way to a cliff that dropped about fifteen feet straight down to the water's edge. From his position he could see a boat in the distance that he believed was the one he had been following. He could also see a small pier that ran out into the sea near the house. A man walked around in the yard and appeared to be calling to his dogs. One by one he corralled three large dogs in a fenced area off to the side of the house away from where a boat would dock. It could be a nightly routine, but Clint guessed the man was expecting visitors.

With the dark trees close behind him, Clint didn't think anyone would notice him, but he decided to squat down in case someone was watching the shore from the boat. At the moment, the distance to the boat also made someone seeing him improbable, but as it came closer, he would either have to get in a prone position of move back into the trees.

He wondered why Deer had told him to follow the boat. What did she expect him to do? The secrecy of Section and his involvement with it had always been top priority, not rescuing people. Nor had she told him to make any effort at rescuing them. Yet, she did send him after them tonight without any specific order to not make contact. The more Clint thought about it, the more he thought she had left the final steps he would take up to him.

Clint had come prepared this time. Maybe from some sixth sense or just a lifetime of experience, he had brought his Beretta and a few other useful items with him tonight.

The boat came closer and began its turn to shore.

Chapter 36

"We're slowing down," Hideki said.

"Yes. I think we'll discover right away whether they intend to let us go or not," Maurice said.

"You know they won't."

"I know." Maurice wanted to repeat that they couldn't give up, but deep down, he knew their situation was hopeless.

As the engine cut off, they could hear movement and voices outside. The boat bumped against something and soon came to a complete stop.

The two men looked at each other. Both too afraid to talk. They waited for the door to open. When it did, Maurice still jumped.

One of the armed guards motioned them to come out. Maurice took a deep breath and forced his feet to move, leaving the room first. He saw the large man but didn't expect the violent push that sent him forward sprawling on the deck. The man kicked him in the ribs. Maurice felt like the kick broke one or more of his ribs. The man leaned over and grabbed Maurice by the arm and yanked him to his feet. One of the guards poked Maurice with the end of his rifle to encourage him to keep moving.

Stepping off the boat onto the pier made Maurice wince in pain. He put his hand against the ribs on the right side of his body in a fruitless attempt to lessen the pain. He saw the man backhand Hideki with such force that he fell backwards. The guard next to Maurice prodded him with his rifle again and shouted at him. Maurice didn't understand the Greek, but he knew the guard wanted him to keep walking. He did.

A grungy-looking man with a white beard and a slightly hunched back stood a few yards off to the side from where the pier ended on land. He held a shotgun and gave Maurice a menacing grin as he got close. Maurice heard the nearby dogs but didn't look around for them. He kept telling himself to keep his wits about him, but the fog of terror overwhelmed his attempt to stay focused.

The guard next to him barked another order. This one only spoke Greek; however, Maurice understood from the guard motioning with his rifle that he was to continue walking toward the house. A pole light near the pier and one by the house provided enough light for Maurice to follow the well-trampled path. He took a quick peek backwards and saw Hideki following him. He thought he saw blood on Hideki's face.

The big brute, who had pushed him down and kicked him, walked out in front of him and led them around the side of the house to an outbuilding. He opened a sliding door and motioned to Maurice to enter. He did, and someone switched on the lone lightbulb hanging from the ceiling. The building looked like an oversized metal shed used for storage. The one exception being a cage placed against the wall to his right. The cage was big enough for a large animal or for storing more valuable items like cases of expensive whiskey or boxes of televisions. Or people, Maurice thought with a shudder.

The guards pushed and prodded Maurice and Hideki into the cage, and the big guy padlocked them in. They all left, turning off the light behind them.

"I liked our last prison better," Maurice said, surprising himself he could talk.

"What are they going to do?" Hideki asked. His voice gave away his fear.

"I don't know," Maurice said. He believed they would never leave the shed alive but didn't want to say the words out loud.

"We're standing on straw, and it stinks. Think other prisoners have been here?"

"Let's hope that smell is from animals and not from other people. They lined the floor with straw only in this cage. The rest of the floor out there is plywood."

"Why haven't they killed us already?" Hideki asked.

"I don't know. Maybe they were supposed to report they got us here safely. We may have to wait here until the guy who had Dean murdered arrives."

"So much for our planning."

"Let's don't give up," Maurice said.

"We had our chance when we were outside, but we didn't do anything."

"We didn't have the opportunity. Do you still have your nail?"

Hideki touched his pants pocket. "Yes, our secret weapon hasn't been of much use yet. Are you surprised they haven't tied us up?"

"Actually I am. They are overconfident."

"They do have guns, and we don't. I'm worried for Kim and Melody," Hideki said.

"Me, too." Maurice wondered how that popped out of Hideki's mouth. While, he didn't disagree, he had had no time to worry about anyone else but himself and maybe Hideki ever since they were put on the boat.

"I can't help but think they are going to be sold into slavery. Remember, that's what the guy said."

"I remember. I just don't want to think about it. Did you hear the dogs?"

"Of course."

"How many do you think there are?"

"Three," Hideki said.

He sounded certain, so Maurice didn't ask him why.

"Did you see if the boat stayed or left?"

"I think it stayed. We may be able to hear its motor if it leaves while we're in here. Does it make a difference?"

"Yes, we need to have different avenues of escape. The boat would be the easiest," Maurice said.

"I think we need to get out of this cage first."

"See if you can pick the lock with the nail," Maurice said.

Hideki looked like he wanted to say something. Instead, he stood up and started to fiddle with the lock. He had only been trying for about ten seconds when the door slid open and a guard walked in. He turned on the light.

"What do you have in your hand?" the guard who spoke English asked.

"Nothing," Hideki said.

"Don't be stupid. I was watching you through the window."

Both Maurice and Hideki turned their heads and saw a small widow they hadn't noticed before.

"Toss it over here, or I'll have to tell Eddy. The least he'll do is break every finger on your hand."

"Is Eddy the big guy?" Hideki asked.

"Yes."

Hideki tossed the nail at the guard.

"Smart decision. If you're lucky you will die quickly. Personally, I hope that's what will happen. But that's up to Eddy and the boss, not me. The last one they brought here they let the dogs kill. That was the worst one I've seen. I'll hope for the best for you."

The guard turned and left the building. He left the nail on the ground and the light on.

"Guess that makes it definite."

"We've got to get out of here," Hideki said. He started checking the chain link cage for any weak or broken spots.

Maurice decided to help him. Between the two, though, they failed to find any part of the cage that was not intact.

Maurice started moving the layer of straw on the floor around with his feet.

"What are you checking for?" Hideki asked.

"A trap door maybe. This layer of straw is at least three inches thick."

Hideki joined in the search but they found nothing. The two men sat down on the straw.

"I guess we need to pray for a miracle," Hideki said.

Chapter 37

Clint watched as the two men in white clothing were marched off the boat and around the side of the house. A few minutes later, some of the men came back into view. The men in white did not reappear with them. The group paused for a second before splitting up. The big man and one of the armed men went into the house.

The dogs began barking, and Clint heard someone shout at the dogs. The dogs went silent. Well trained, Clint thought. Dogs always heightened the threat, especially well-trained guard dogs.

The older man with the beard and one of the armed men walked back to a point near the boat. These two started smoking and talking. Clint could only hear bits and pieces of the conversation, but he wouldn't have understood them anyway. The fence ran to the edge of the cliff. The last pole had to be positioned about ten inches from the edge to allow room for the cement foundation. Clint believed he could squeeze around it without making any noise or falling.

He debated his plan for less than ten seconds. She told him to follow the boat. While his mission wasn't to rescue anyone, did she really expect him to watch them die? Besides, he thought, his target could be in that house. He had anticipated that things might turn hot and had come prepared.

Clint removed his black Covid mask from a jacket pocket and put it on. He also removed a tube of black makeup and wiped some under his eyes. He pulled his black stocking cap lower onto his forehead. Next, he attached the noise suppressor, or silencer as the movies referred to them, to his Beretta. He would have to get a lot closer for his weapon to be of any use.

He edged around the end of the fence, and staying low to the ground, he moved toward the men by the boat. The two men weren't standing guard. Clint watched them as he narrowed the distance to them. They were laughing and slapping each other on the arm. Another man appeared on the boat and said something to the duo that made them laugh some more.

Clint thought this new person had to be the boat captain. He also raised the odds against Clint getting close enough for his pistol to be effective. The man on the boat faced the direction that had Clint in its view. Whatever the two had said had riled the captain sufficiently that his attention solely focused on the two men on shore. He shouted something at them and raised both hands in disgust. With the three men distracted, Clint increased his speed and closed in on the trio.

The boat captain started to turn away when he must have seen Clint. He stopped and said something to the two on the land.

The two men glanced in Clint's direction but then turned back to ask something of the man on the boat. The boat captain then pointed at Clint and shouted a warning. The two turned and brought up their weapons. Clint dove to the ground just as the shotgun blasted dozens of birdshot pellets in his direction.

On the ground, Clint not only became a smaller target, it enabled him to shoot back from a prone position. Using the ground to help stabilize one's aim, the prone position normally increases a shooter's accuracy. In this case, it did just that.

Clint's first shot hit the man with the shotgun in the chest. He didn't see the impact, but he saw his target's hand reach for his chest when he collapsed to the ground. The man next to him had not yet started shooting. He may have thought Clint had been hit by the shotgun. Whatever the reason, Clint didn't hesitate and fired his second round into the man.

The man on the boat had disappeared, so Clint fired another shot at his second target. He had staggered back a step or two but had not fallen. The second round caused this man to drop to the ground next to his partner. Clint saw the man on the boat reappear with a handgun of some sort and move toward the edge of the boat to get the boat's light behind him. Unfortunately for him, his eyes had to readjust, and in those few seconds, Clint raced another five yards closer before once again diving to the ground.

Clint aimed and fired off two rounds into the man. The man slid down behind the side of the boat. Feeling confident that he had hit him, Clint ran up to the fallen men on the ground first. They were both dead or close to it. Clint tossed their weapons into the water. He crept down the pier.

He hesitated, not wanting to peer over the edge of the boat and get shot in the head. Fortunately, he saw the man's leg first. The way it sprawled out indicated the captain was lying on his stomach with his head away from Clint. Knowing it was a position from which it would be very difficult for the man to shoot him, Clint walked quickly to the boat and looked over the side. Enough blood had spread out over the deck to convince Clint that this man posed no threat.

The others must have heard the shotgun being fired, but

Clint doubted they heard his shots. He looked toward the house but saw no movement. The dogs were barking again, but everything else seemed peaceful. Not a good sign, he thought. Rather than get pinned on the boat, Clint ran along the water's edge for about twenty yards and squatted behind a large propane tank that sat horizontally on the ground. One end faced the house and the other the sea. The light from the pole near the pier barely reached him. Not the best place to hide in a gun fight, he thought, but his plan didn't include anyone shooting at him.

Someone shouted from the back door of the house. Clint didn't understand him, but he knew the guy wanted to know what was going on. He should've only heard the one shot. That might have surprised those in the house, but since they didn't hear any more shooting, they may not have been overly concerned. The old man may have taken a shot at a fox or some other critter in the yard.

Still, a man had stepped out into the yard and started to walk in the direction of the boat. He carried a rifle of some sort that Clint couldn't identify in the semi-darkness. The propane tank sat directly behind the house while the pier was now off to Clint's left. The man's path to the boat would take him close by Clint. At some point along the way, the man would recognize the two lumps on the ground were bodies. Clint hoped he wouldn't do so too soon.

Clint took his eyes off the man long enough to look for anyone else outside the house. He could see an outbuilding next to the house off to the side, but no people moving about. Not counting the two prisoners, Clint had counted six men. Three were down and a fourth now walked in front of him.

That left the big guy and one more armed man. Other people could have been in the house, but he would deal with that later.

The man stopped walking and crouched. He brought his rifle up into a shooting position. Clint now recognized it as a military style automatic rifle, maybe another AR-15, like the one he had just tossed into the water. Clint stayed still. He needed the man's focus to go back to the bodies on the ground or to the house, if he started calling for help.

After a quick glance around the man stood up and stared at the bodies. He called out a name and took a tentative step toward the pier. He kept the rifle in the ready position but pointed at the bodies.

Clint stepped away from the propane tank. He kept his Beretta aimed at his target as he walked quietly at him. The closer the better. The man's tunnel vision on the bodies allowed Clint to get within five yards before the man noticed him. He spun around quicker than Clint expected. Clint put two quick rounds in the man's chest, but the man still managed to squeeze the trigger firing off a dozen or so rounds as he fell backwards. The rounds went high hitting nothing but air. Clint instinctively ducked and ran to the side of the house away from any windows.

The automatic gunfire would've gotten everyone's attention for at least a mile or two. He thought he heard someone shout, but the noise from the shooting had momentarily deafened him. The lights in the house went out. At least one person was still in there. Clint moved quietly alongside the house staying low. He checked for open windows as he went. As he rounded the corner to the front, he paused and reloaded his Beretta. He knew he had a couple rounds left, but better safe than sorry, he thought. He peeked into a window by the front door but saw no one.

He bypassed the front door. They would expect him to come in through a door. He made it to another corner of the house and stopped. He could see the outbuilding. It could be a small barn or a very large shed. Clint guessed the two men in the white clothing would be in there. They would have to wait.

He also saw the large dog kennel. For whatever reason, the dogs were now silent.

He crept along the side of the house, keeping an eye on the other building. Everything remained still. He could hear the small waves hitting the shore. As he neared a window, smaller than the others, he noticed it was cracked open about an inch.

Clint stood up high enough to look through the window and saw an empty bathroom. He slid the window up as far as it would go. The opening was small, but he thought he could squeeze through it. The trick would be to make as little noise as possible and to get through before someone discovered him. If he had more time, he would wait for different options, but he didn't. Reinforcements could be on the way, or even worse, the police may be enroute. He did not want to be discovered.

He wondered if his priorities were screwed up as he climbed and shimmied himself into the bathroom.

Chapter 38

Both Maurice and Hideki jumped when they heard the gunshot. They heard their guard shout something outside.

"Sounded like the old man's shotgun," Maurice said.

"Hopefully, they all kill each other," Hideki said.

"Wouldn't that be something, but I think he just shot as some stray animal. It would be nice if there was a rescue attempt going on right now. More shooting would be needed for that though."

Hideki nodded. He looked at the small window and saw their guard looking in at them. Maurice followed his eyes and saw the guard, too.

"Well, I guess he wasn't shot," Maurice said.

"Too bad."

The dogs were barking.

"Ever been bitten by a dog?" Maurice asked.

"No, why even ask that?"

"Sorry."

"Were you?" Hideki asked after a moment.

"Yes, when I was a teenager. It hurt. That's why we only have a cat."

"We don't have any pets, well, except for our fish. Do fish really count as pets? You can't pet them."

Maurice smiled. "I've heard that before, but yes, I would think they could be thought of as pets. When I was little, my friend had a pet turtle."

"My friend, Sasha, had three beautiful cats. At least his wife has those to comfort her. I hope my fish will comfort my family."

"Don't be negative. We aren't dead yet,"

The two men looked at each other. Neither saw any hope left in the other. They sat without speaking for a minute, before a series of rapid gunfire interrupted the silence. They both jerked their hands up to their faces.

"What was that?" Maurice murmured.

The guard outside shouted something. He then opened the door and hurried inside before sliding it shut. He moved to the window and peered outside.

"Visitors?" Maurice said.

"Be quiet," the guard ordered. He looked through the window first one way and then moved to the other side of the window to look the other way.

"He can't see past the house," Maurice whispered.

The guard turned and looked at them. "Who is out there?"

"Are you asking us? How would we know. We don't even know where we are. We haven't talked to anyone since we were kidnapped," Hideki said.

"Maybe it's the Marines," Maurice said. He started giggling.

"Stop it! Now!"

"Yes, yes," Maurice said. He didn't know why he was giggling, although he knew his emotions were running wild.

"Shouldn't you go out to check?" Hideki asked.

"No, I'm supposed to stay here," the guard said.

"We can't protect you if we stay in this cage," Maurice said.

The guard looked at him and sneered. He then turned his attention to what was happening outside the window. He continued to move around to get better angles but gave no indication to either of the two prisoners that he ever saw anything. After thirty seconds, the guard walked over to the cage.

"Why do they want to kill you?" he asked.

"You don't know?" Maurice asked.

"No? They kept you, they fed you, you worked for them, so why do they now want to kill you?"

Both prisoners shrugged their shoulders.

"Are they going to kill the two women?" the guard asked.

"You should know more than we do," Maurice said.

"They don't tell us. We just do what we're told. We have no choice either. Are you from Japan?"

"Yes," Hideki said.

"I would like to visit there. Maybe America one day, too. I learned my English working for the American air base near Athens."

"We are in Greece," Hideki said, confirming what they had already guessed.

"Yes, did no one tell you?"

"No one told us anything," Maurice said. He almost started feeling sorry for the guard. He guessed the guard was in his late twenties.

"Strange."

"Have you ever seen anyone get killed?" Maurice asked. He hadn't forgotten the guard's earlier comments, but he thought thinking and talking more about it might keep the guard distracted.

"Only a few times. If you work for the boss and Eddy, you see people get killed. They are very dangerous men."

"Is Eddy the big guy?"

"Yes."

"Who is the boss?" Hideki asked, getting into the discussion.

The guards shook his head and didn't say anything. He went back to the window and stopped talking.

"I pushed him too far," Hideki whispered.

"That's okay, nothing to lose," Maurice said.

"Something must be going on out there. That guy is scared to go back outside."

Maurice silently prayed that help had arrived.

Chapter 39

Clint stood still in the bathroom for a full thirty seconds. He made more noise than he wanted while struggling to get through the window. The bathroom door, an inch shy of being totally closed, should have helped keep the sound from spreading too far. As he waited, he heard nothing to indicate someone else might be in the house. He wondered if they had all gone outside to investigate the gunfire.

He opened the door enough to peer out and saw nothing but a short, dark hallway. From where he was, he couldn't identify the type of room at the end of the hall. He walked quietly out of the bathroom.

The big man pounced when Clint reached the room. Eddy had been hiding at the corner and moved quicker than Clint had expected. He grabbed the Beretta, nearly wrenching it from Clint's hand.

Both had a death grip on the weapon. Clint head butted his attacker, but Eddy kept maneuvering to get better leverage on the Beretta. They were pressed against each other. Suddenly, the man changed tactics and pushed Clint ahead of him in three quick steps, crushing him against a wall.

Clint slammed into the wall, with Eddy's full weight thrust into him at the same time. In a burst of strength, Eddy managed to yank Clint's pistol away. Eddy took a step back, but rather than shoot Clint, he tossed the weapon to a far corner of the room. He tried to drive his fist into Clint's face, but Clint managed to slip the punch and drove two quick jabs into the man's face.

Clint moved to his left getting his back off the wall. He knew he was granted a new lease on life when the man hadn't shot him. The only reason that he could think of was that his opponent had extreme confidence in his ability to outfight anyone. Stupid, Clint thought, but it also meant the guy was still very dangerous.

Eddy charged Clint, and Clint reacted. Eddy stood an inch taller than Clint and had him by at least twenty pounds. Although Clint didn't know it, Eddy had been a street fighter, a brawler, and a bully his entire life. He relied on his brute strength and intimidation, never feeling mercy for his opponent.

On the other hand, Clint had nearly two decades of training, practice, and experience. Despite the confined space, Clint managed to parry and counterattack, keeping his opponent off him. When Eddy did get a grip, Clint twisted and bent fingers or hands or gouged at eyes to break away.

Eddy stopped trying to grab Clint and started swinging wide, roundhouse punches. Clint deflected most of them, but when they did connect, they hurt. Clint landed a number of jabs and a straight right punch, bloodying Eddy's nose and lips. The big man seemed unfazed, staying on offense. A large ring on Eddy's finger flashed close to Clint's face more than once.

Clint kept moving, and when he had enough space, he kicked at his opponent's right knee. The kick connected, but rather than go down, Eddy grunted and managed to grab Clint's ankle. He jerked Clint's leg to him and seized Clint's jacket at the waist. Clint chopped at Eddy's nose, striking it at an angle. Blood spurted immediately out of it. The broken nose did little to slow the man. He lifted Clint off his feet, spun, and threw Clint against a wall.

Clint smashed into the wall and dropped hard to the floor. He felt like he had the wind knocked out of him. He forced himself to roll to the side and avoided a size fourteen boot that smashed into the wall inches from his head. Clint moved as fast as he could on his hands and feet while gasping to inhale air. He noticed the big man stagger backwards as his injured right knee almost gave out on him.

The few seconds respite gave Clint a new plan. He stayed on the ground and crawled toward the opening to another room. The big guy did what Clint expected and moved to block his escape.

Eddy looked down at Clint. He grinned and grabbed a wooden chair, one of the few pieces of furniture in the room. He roared, just like a lion might roar before closing to kill wounded prey. Clint crawled backwards into a corner of the room much like a terrified victim might. Eddy took two steps toward him and raised the chair off to his side.

For a moment, Clint had a strange urge to wait and see how his opponent planned on using the chair. He was too tall to swing the chair over his head. Yet, Clint knew he was in no position to delay what needed to be done. He reached behind him and grabbed the Beretta off the floor. He pulled the trigger four times before the man in front of him sank to the floor.

Clint remained where he was for a full minute. The man had hurt him, and he needed time to get his breath and his focus back. If anyone else was in the house, they would have made an appearance by now. The prisoners could be upstairs locked in a room, although he expected they were in the out building.

He stood up, and after ensuring his opponent had died, Clint rifled through Eddy's pockets. He removed a set of keys, guessing he would have any important ones. After he picked up his cap, he checked out the rest of the house. The old house had several rooms, but other than the dining room and a couple bedrooms the rest of the house was unfurnished. He considered contacting Section but decided to wait. He knew he had been lucky to have gotten this far, but there was no reason to pass on an incomplete report of the night's events.

Before leaving the house, Clint looked out windows on each side of the house to see if he could see anyone else moving about. He didn't see anyone, but he knew by his earlier count, one more man with a rifle had to be out there somewhere.

He went out the front door. The dogs had started barking again, but not as much as they had earlier. Otherwise, the night was silent. He moved to the corner and looked at the building. He thought he saw a face looking out a small window, but it disappeared after a second or two.

He counted to ten, and when the face didn't reappear, he raced to the building. Bracing himself against the outside wall, he listened and heard talking. To his surprise the people inside were speaking in English.

Clint watched as the sliding door opened a few inches and stopped. The voices from inside became clearer. They were talking about a bear or something that hurt people. He half listened while he once again studied the surroundings for any other signs of life.

Chapter 40

"Hear that roar," the guard said to his two captives.

"Was that what that was?" Maurice asked.

"That was Eddy. Someone is getting his ass kicked. I've heard him do that a few times before. He's disabled his opponent and is going in for the kill. Might not kill them though. He might just break some bones, you know, smash up a face. I saw him take two guys on at once in a bar. Beat them both to an inch of their lives. He made that roar then. It's quite scary to be there."

"Who would he be hurting here?" Hideki asked.

"Likely the person who fired off the shots a minute ago. The boss has rules about that."

"Is the boss here?" Hideki asked.

"No, just Eddy. The boss must have given him instructions. Of course, he could show up later. Might be better for you if he doesn't."

"Why is that?" Maurice asked. He didn't really want to know, but having the conversation kept his mind from dwelling on death. He thought he heard something outside the building.

The guard did, too. He stopped talking and went to look out the window. After a couple seconds, he moved to the sliding door and cracked it open an inch.

"I wouldn't go out there," Maurice said.

The guard looked back at him.

"Shut up."

"I'm serious. Let Eddy handle it. If you go out there and shoot at something in a panic, you'll have to face Eddy. You just said he was beating the crap out of someone for doing that, didn't you?" Maurice said.

The guard shouted something in Greek through the small opening in the doorway. No one answered him. He mumbled something to himself.

"If it's the police, wouldn't it be better if you gave up and let us go? We will tell the police that you treated us well," Hideki said.

"One thing, I know for sure, that's not the police. At least not the local city police," the guard said and then seemed to think about something.

Maurice suspected the guard was considering the possibility the national police may have shown up. Something was happening out there, and from the guard's behavior, it wasn't anything he expected.

"Let us out," Maurice said again.

"I can't. I don't have a key, so quit asking me."

For some reason, that surprised Maurice. He had assumed the guard would have access to the key.

"Listen, I have a different question for you," Hideki said.

The guard looked back at the two in the cage.

"What did they do with all the information we gave them?" Hideki asked.

"What?"

"They kidnapped us, tormented us, threatened our families, and had us recommend improvements to an Israeli drone. Do you know what they did with the information?"

"I don't know. Why would I know? Don't you?"

"No, they didn't tell us either. That's why we don't understand why they now want to kill us. We don't know where we are, who any of you are, or what you did with the information we furnished. We can't cause any trouble," Hideki said.

The guard slid the door open several more inches. "I'm sorry. I don't know any more than you do. I feel sorrier for the two women. I know the boss has already hurt them. I can't imagine what he has planned for them now that he is done with you."

"How did you get involved with him?" Maurice asked.

"It just happened."

"Shouldn't you have heard from Eddy by now?" Maurice wanted to keep the guard worrying. "It seems strange that it's quiet out there and that no one from your group has responded to your shouts."

"Are there any bears around here?" Hideki sounded serious, but Maurice wondered if he was just playing with the guard's mind.

"Deeper in the mountains there are a few, but not here," the guard said.

"That could explain why we've heard gunshots and why it is quiet now. Could that roar have been a bear's growl. Eddy might be tough, but against a bear?" Hideki raised his eyebrows.

"Be quiet. You don't know anything. If there was a bear, we would have heard someone screaming. Do you think a person would be silent as a bear ripped them apart? You two have not seen the real world."

Maurice doubted if the guard had ever witnessed someone

being mauled by a bear. More likely, he might have seen someone tortured and heard the screams.

"Well, if you are going out there, be careful," Maurice said. For some strange reason, he half meant it.

"What?" Hideki whispered to him, again raising his eyebrows.

The guard slid the door open wide enough to step outside. Maurice watched him look around. The guard suddenly gasped. He started to bring his rifle up and around when he staggered backwards. He managed to fire off a single round before stumbling backwards into the building. Hunching over, he tried to say something before falling to the ground in front of them.

The next thing Maurice saw surprised him even more. A man dressed in all black streaked through the doorway, did a roll on the ground, and popped up in a kneeling position, sweeping the room with his eyes. A pistol of some sort swept the room along with his eyes.

His eyes returned to the cage and the two prisoners. His face was covered with the kind of cloth mask many people wore to prevent the spread of Covid. Maurice had a strange desire to tell him the cloth masks weren't very effective.

"Are you two okay?" the man asked. He wore a stocking cap that was pulled down close to his eyes. Black face paint underlined his eyes.

Hideki started crying.

Chapter 41

Clint crouched down and waited for the man to come outside or move further inside. He didn't have to wait long. The door slid open and a man carrying a rifle stepped outside. The man looked around and spotted Clint. He started to swing the weapon to aim, and Clint shot him twice in the chest. The man fired one shot into the air before he backed into the building and fell.

Not knowing for sure that there wasn't another guard inside, Clint raced into the building and rolled into a firing position. The maneuver was meant to make him a hard target to hit, but proved unnecessary. The two men in white, whom he had previously seen, were standing inside a large cage.

"Are you two okay?"

The two prisoners stared at him and said nothing. Clint recognized the two from the photos he had seen. The Japanese scientist started crying.

"How do we get you out of there?"

"Are you really here to rescue us?" Maurice said.

"I'm not here to harm you. Is there a key here somewhere?"

"I don't know. He said he didn't have one, but he could've been lying. They were going to kill us, so I doubt he would've felt guilty about lying. He did say the big ogre had the keys. Did you run into him?"

Clint unzipped a jacket pocket and pulled out the set of keys he had taken from Eddy. "Yes, and he did have some keys in his pocket. Here," Clint said and walked to the cage, handing the keys to Maurice. "I need to check outside again."

"Don't leave us," Maurice said.

"I'll be back. How many men were here?"

"Counting the boat captain, five men brought us here and one man met us. If there were more, we didn't see them," Maurice said.

"Thank you, thank you," Hideki said, getting his composure back.

Clint walked outside and looked around. Six men were all he counted, too. They were all dead and accounted for. He had checked the house after his altercation with the big man inside and found no one.

Although he didn't expect to find anyone else, Clint returned to the house. Once he double checked to be sure the house was empty, he took a picture of Eddy and what he believed to be his driver's license.

He went to the boat for a quick inspection. When Clint returned to the outbuilding, he found the two men out of the cage but still inside.

"Is it safe?" Maurice asked.

"For now."

"Who are you?" Hideki asked.

"Don't worry about who I am. Let's get you out of here."

"Yes, let's do," Maurice said.

"Do you have a car?" Hideki asked.

"No, you need to use the same mode of transportation you took to get here. I hope one of you can drive a boat."

"I can," Hideki said.

"Good, let's go," Clint said and led the duo to the pier.

"My God, are they dead?" Maurice asked he saw the bodies

on the ground.

"Yes."

"Did you ....?" Hideki said.

"Kill them, yes. They shot at me first."

"I heard the pistol," Hideki said.

"On the boat," Clint said and motioned with his free hand. He still maintained a grip on the Beretta with his right hand.

The two didn't hesitate.

"Oh!" Maurice said upon seeing the dead boat captain.

"My suggestion is to throw him and his pistol overboard right here. A bucket or two of water can rinse the blood off. There's a bucket up there. That will delay a police overreaction. Also, keys are in the ignition."

The two looked at each other, but within seconds lifted the dead man up and dropped him over the side. The pistol splashed into the water a few seconds later.

"Are you not coming with us?" Hideki asked while Maurice hung the bucket over the side of the boat to fill it.

"No, and please don't give them a very good description of me. I shouldn't be here."

"What? You had to be here. We all prayed for someone to come. They were going to kill us," Maurice said.

"So, what should we tell everyone?" Hideki asked.

"The truth about everything. Just one white lie, don't give them a good description of me. Agree between yourselves how you want to describe me, so your stories match."

"We can do that. Which way do we go?" Hideki was smiling now.

"Follow the coast that way," Clint pointed in the direction they had come. "Stay about a half mile off shore. You'll run into a big city in about a half hour or so. Go past the first group of big building you see, unless you want to go back to where you just came from."

Hideki shook his head.

"Follow the city lights for about a mile and you'll see a large harbor area. Work your way in there and call the US or Japanese Embassy. I wouldn't hang around this boat long. It might be recognized, and the wrong folks might show up to claim it."

"Do you have a phone we could use?" Maurice asked. He had finished pouring water onto the deck.

"Better yet, there's a phone next to the captain's chair and a wallet with enough money to keep you in food until help arrives. Use them, they owe you."

"You sure you don't want to come with us?" Maurice asked.

"No, I can't. Feel free to call home with that phone, too."

"Is someone rescuing Melody and Kim, too?" Hideki asked.

"Let's hope so. What about the other man?"

"Who?" Maurice asked.

"Dean."

"They killed him. They were going to kill us," Maurice said again.

"Good luck," Clint said and walked away into the darkness. The news about Dean didn't surprise him. Seconds later, he heard the boat startup. He looked back and saw it pull away from the pier. He imagined one or both were already trying to call their wives.

He waited until he reached the motorcycle before he called Section. Deer answered and started talking before he had a chance to say anything.

"I've been worried about you."

"Things got dicey but went better than expected. Two male scientists are on their way back to Thessaloniki alone by boat as we speak. The kidnappers had already killed Dean."

"Are you okay?"

"Yes."

"Did they see you?"

At least this time she asked the two questions in the right order, Clint thought and smiled. "Not enough to describe me. I wore a Covid mask and a stocking cap pulled down low. They were so happy to be set free, they promised not to give a good description of what they did see of me. I believe they will, they owe me."

"Good. Did they have any idea where the two women might be?"

"No. They were concerned about them, but they knew nothing," Clint said.

"Do you expect a police response any time soon?"

"No. The two scientists didn't know where they were other than to say a couple miles up the coast."

"Finding and freeing the two men was a good break, but rescuing them or the two women is not your objective."

"I know. I thought my target might have been with them," Clint said.

"Makes sense, and like I said, it was a good break that you were able to free them. We always believed they were going to kill the scientists when they were done with them."

"I'm sending you a photo of one of the men I encountered here. I believe he is one of Agape's deputies."

"Okay, keep your head down. Hold on a second."

The phone went silent for a second. Clint sent the photos before he started rolling the motorcycle back to the dirt trail that would take him back out to the road.

"We've got something interesting happening. I'll get back to you in a few minutes," Deer said and ended the call.

Clint rode back to the paved road and headed toward Thessaloniki. The cool night air felt good. He could feel the tension in his muscles fade away. Only one old, dilapidated pickup truck passed him going the other way before he saw the lights of the city.

Once in the city, he slowed and kept his speed just under the limit. No reason to attract anyone's attention, especially a roving police vehicle. The call came in from Buzz just as he was getting off the motorcycle in the hotel parking lot.

"Are you in bed yet?" Buzz asked.

"In a few minutes, but you probably know that," Clint said and grinned to himself. He would bet a month's paycheck that Buzz had been monitoring his movements for the last hour or so.

"We need you to head toward Volos right now. It's not that far, but we believe that your target is heading there now. He's likely in a van and has the two women with him."

"How am I supposed to find him?"

"I'm sending you GPS coordinates to a small town on the coast. It has a dock where small boats can pull up to. It's mostly a fishing town, but we have reason to believe a nasty guy from North Africa has arranged with Agape to meet him there in, what is it, just over two hours from now. From our intercepts, it sounds like he is going to trade something for two women."

"No one else interested in helping out?"

"We just got this. There's no time, and we weren't supposed to get the information as fast as we did. Plus, you know the other agencies would have to mull the information over for a day or two before sharing it or acting on it."

Clint knew he was right.

"Listen, we can get someone else to rescue the women. They won't go far. They'll be traveling by boat. Your target is Agape. We've already got some intel indicating that he has been contacted to use his drones to go after a Western industrial leader. I also believe he will disappear once he finds out what happened tonight. We may never find him again."

"I understand," Clint said.

"It's going to be a late night."

"I'm okay."

"Stay safe, my friend," Buzz said.

Clint drove to a nearby gas station and topped off the motorcycle's tank. He checked his phone for the text from Buzz with the GPS location. It automatically fed into the phone's map. The trip should take him just over two hours. No time to waste, he thought. With any luck he would get there and get back before sunrise. He planned to spend tomorrow in bed.

Chapter 42

The bang on the door frightened Melody and brought her out of her already fitful sleep. She sat up, clutching the sheet and blanket to her. The door opened, and a guard switched on the light to her room.

"Get dressed. You leave in five minutes," he said in broken English.

"What? Where?"

The guard closed the door without answering. Left alone, Melody got out of bed and started dressing. Both fear and hope flooded her emotions. Leaving? Where would they be taking her. Leaving didn't sound like dying, but did it mean being set free?

She remembered someone said she wouldn't be killed. What had they said? The women would be sold. Fear raced back in and took charge of her emotions. They intended to sell her.

"I won't allow it. I'd rather be dead," she said aloud to the empty room.

The door swung open and two guards rushed in and seized her. Her hands were tied behind her and a bag made of some fabric pulled over her head.

"What are you doing to me?"

A hand yanked at her arm. She tried to resist and someone punched her hard in the stomach. She collapsed to one knee. The guards grabbed her by her armpits and dragged her out of the room.

"Walk! Or we will hurt you," one of the guards who spoke English said from somewhere further down the hallway. She had only encountered two guards who spoke English, and Melody tried to put a face with the voice she just heard.

She started walking with one guard guiding her by the arm. A few seconds later she heard Kim's muffled sobs.

"Kim, are you alright?"

"No, what are they going to do?"

"Shut up," the guard ordered.

Both women did.

"You are lucky you are not dead like the other two."

"What is going to happen to us?" Melody asked.

"I don't know. I don't, so you can quit asking me. We were told to take you to the van. I don't even know if we're going with you or not."

"Are we going home?" Kim asked.

She didn't get an answer.

Melody wanted to believe that. They might still blindfold them with a bag and bind their hands before taking them somewhere to release them, but she knew deep down that wasn't going to happen. Once the guard said the two others had been killed, she knew they wouldn't set her free.

They hadn't walked far before they stopped. She could hear doors sliding open, and they got into what she soon realized was an elevator. They went up for less than ten seconds, before getting off and walking for some distance still inside the building.

"Well, here you two are."

Melody cringed. She imagined Kim did, too. She recognized the voice of the man who had ordered the killing of

Dean. The same man who had raped her.

"Put them in the van," Sonder said in Greek.

Melody didn't understand him and wasn't prepared when one of the guards shoved her forward. She bumped into the back bumper of the van and almost fell forward.

"Get in," Sonder said.

"How?" Melody said in frustration.

Suddenly, hands grabbed her and pushed her in. She felt Kim bump against her as she, too, was roughly tossed into the van. Kim cussed at them, but the van door slammed shut cutting her off.

"Are you okay?" Kim asked.

"Yes. Are we alone?"

They both sat in silence for a moment listening for any other sounds. They could hear the men talking outside the van, but their conversation was in Greek. A van door opened. They could hear a man grunting as he climbed into the van. Then the door shut and the van's engine started up.

"What do you think is happening?" Kim asked.

"I don't know. Do you think Hideki and Maurice are really dead?"

"That's what the guard said. They could be just tormenting us or trying to make us more compliant."

"It's possible, although, I can't believe they are going to set us free. Remember they said they were going to sell us," Melody said.

"Makes me wish I hadn't tried so hard to stay in shape."

Despite their situation, Melody smiled at her remark. "I'm no spring chicken, so they won't get much for me."

"Think we can get these hoods off?"

"Yes. If we can move ourselves where we are back-to-back, one of us can slide down, and the other pull off the hood."

"If someone is in here with us, they'll stop us, but who cares," Kim said.

The two women couldn't see, but they could feel each other as they squirmed around until they were finally sitting back-to-back.

"I'll try and slide down," Kim said.

In a few seconds, Melody felt the cloth hood and gripped it. She pulled her arms up behind her until Kim stopped her.

"You've got my hair, too. Try to grab it in another spot. It's already half off."

Melody did and pulled the hood the rest of the way off.

"It's off, but it's really dark in here. I can barely see anything."

"Get mine off anyway," Melody said.

"I will. We'll have to do it the same way. I can't get my hands in front of me."

"It is dark, but at least I can breathe better," Melody said after Kim had removed her hood.

"There must be a wall between us and the driver. Otherwise, we should be able to see out the front windshield," Kim said.

"We need to get out of here." Melody scooted to the back door and put her face close to it. She looked for a handle that might open the door.

"Be careful. We may need the van to stop or slow down if you're thinking about jumping out."

Melody discovered what she believed was the door handle, but it wouldn't move. Thinking it must be locked, she first looked around and then felt around for a lever or button that might unlock it.

"Damn!"

"What?"

"It's locked, and I can't find the unlock lever," Melody said.

"Let me look." Kim maneuvered herself on her knees as Melody backed away from the door. She failed to do any better than Melody in finding a way to open the back door to the van. She sat back down next to Melody.

"Who would want to buy us?" Kim asked.

"I have no idea. I mean, I don't know much about human trafficking, but everything I've heard or seen, the girls are always quite young. We are not over the hill, but we certainly don't fit the normal picture. I mean, if they had a catalog of girls or women for sale, we certainly wouldn't make the front cover."

Kim laughed. "I shouldn't be laughing. This is not a funny situation we have found ourselves in."

"We have been in an unimaginable situation for weeks. I'm glad we still have the ability to laugh at anything."

"For the record, if I didn't laugh, I'd be crying. I'm terrified, and I'm mad as hell at these people. Who do they think they are?"

"They're terrible people, Jack's boss in particular. He's a psychopath. I will kill him if I get the chance," Melody said.

"Do you think Jack is as bad?"

"No." She couldn't make herself say what she knew, what she saw. She already admitted to being raped, but she couldn't talk about it. Jack's boss raped her and forced Jack to watch. She had closed her eyes and tried to put her mind elsewhere but ended up staring at Jack. She pleaded for help, but Jack just stood there. She hated him for letting that happen to her.

It was an hour later that same night, when she was alone, trying to think of something else or to sleep, that she saw Jack's face again in her mind. She saw it as clearly as she had before. However, now her mind now focused on his face not on what had been happening to her. She saw the tear he quickly wiped away. She saw him start to turn away and stop when his boss shouted at him. Jack had not wanted to be there. He was as much a prisoner as she was. He just didn't know it, or maybe he did and couldn't do anything about it.

Melody didn't understand Greek, but she knew that Jack's boss encouraged Jack to follow his lead and take advantage of her. Jack shook his head. He looked like he was pleading not to have to do it. His boss laughed at him, but they all left.

"I hope you're thinking of a way out of here," Kim said.

"What? Oh sorry, I have a hard time staying focused."

"Me, too. I'd love to find a safe place and just cry all day."

"Me, too." Melody looked at Kim, but it was too dark to see anything but the outline of her face. "We have to find a way to escape before we get to whatever final destination they have planned for us. That may give us days to escape or just a few hours."

"We have to mentally prepare ourselves to take advantage of any opportunity that may come our way. Could you kill someone?"

Melody didn't have to think for very long. "Yes."

The van braked hard, and both women fell forward. They heard the driver curse. After a few seconds the van accelerated, and their journey continued.

"That hurt," Kim said. When the van braked, her momentum caused her to fall sideways. With her hands tied behind her back, she couldn't do anything but fall on the side of her face.

Melody fell backwards and suffered nothing more than a small bump on her head. "Can't do much to protect ourselves with our hands cuffed. I think they used those plastic flex cuffs. Can you chew through those things?"

"I doubt it, but I'm willing to give it a try."

"I'll try to stand," Melody awkwardly stood up. She had to lean forward and bend her head down as she stood about six inches taller than the height of the van's ceiling. "This is definitely not designed for people."

Kim got on her knees behind her. After a few seconds of searching, she managed to get a couple teeth on the plastic band, but that was all.

"No, can't do it. Sorry, Melody."

"That's okay. I imagine they're designed to not be chewable."

"How long do you think we'll be in this van? I mean, I can't think they want to take us to any public place where we could bang on the side of the truck or scream for help. I don't see them letting us out to eat at a café or restaurant."

"Or even at a rest area where there might be other people," Melody said.

"My guess is that we'll get to our destination tonight. It may not be our final destination, but they'll put us in a different type of vehicle or a plane."

"If we are in Greece, it could even be to a boat."

"It sounded like there was just one person, the driver, in the van with us. Maybe we could bribe him to let us go," Kim said.

"Or overpower him. There are two of us, and I'm ready to hurt someone."

"Then we have to hope for a breakdown. I'm sure there will be more of them when we get to wherever we're going."

"I'll pray for a flat tire."

"I hate to say this, Melody, but I'm glad I'm not alone."

"It's not your fault, and I'm glad you're here with me." Melody paused for a second. "What if we're going to be sold off separately."

"You mean like an auction where they bid on us?"

"Yes. I won't stand a chance. I'll either get the low bidder or worse."

"Don't say that. We'll say they have to take us as a team. That we do everything together. They might like that."

To Melody's surprise and despite their situation, her mind focused on Kim's lack of rebuttal. She hadn't remarked that someone might not pay more for her.

Chapter 43

Clint slowed as the highway slid by the city of Volos. He enjoyed traveling by motorcycle, and he wondered why he hadn't bought one since he sold his last one fifteen years earlier. He would not buy the same model he had rented, but the rental choices were few. He would want a larger engine, for sure. However, this one had enough power to go the speed limit, and that was all he hoped he would need.

Traffic remained light as he approached his destination. The mountains that covered most of the center of Greece ran closer to the sea here. He turned off the highway onto a narrow, two-lane paved road. He stopped a little under a mile from his destination, pulling off on what looked like a well-worn, dirt parking area for trucks.

He could see the sea in the distance and closer in, he saw a dozen or so lights from the small fishing village Buzz had mentioned. Using his binoculars, he located the pier. A dozen or so fishing boats were anchored nearby. He wondered if someone slept on the boats, or if a water taxi took the crews back and forth.

The pier looked as though it was a few hundred yards south of the town. A road ran from it and split with one road going along the shoreline to town and the other appeared to circumvent the town. Clint couldn't be sure as his view was blocked. Further out in the water, he saw a boat that appeared to be coming toward the town.

Clint steered the motorcycle to a spot behind a billboard

advertising beer. No one had driven by since he had stopped, but he knew he didn't want to be spotted by anyone who might. He called Buzz.

"Hey, Clint, I see you're about there."

"Yes. I see a boat coming in. Should I be interested in it?"

"See any other boats coming toward you?"

Clint couldn't see anything from where he was, but he knew he hadn't seen anything else in the water. "No, just the one."

"How close can you get to the pier or to anywhere else they may pull up to?"

"Not sure yet, but I might be able to get close."

"Deer is regretting not having a sniper rifle in place for you."

Clint had no idea how she could have pulled that off. He didn't comment on Buzz's remark.

"We have good information that a nasty group of people have paid a fair chunk of money for the two women scientists. They have arranged to pick them up in about twenty minutes at your location. At the same meeting, we believe Sonder Agape and a senior member of this other cartel or faction will be having a brief meeting."

"Wouldn't this be something the Agency or the locals should be interested in?" Clint asked.

"No time. Like I said, we only were able to piece this together a few hours ago. They have the same information we do, but they haven't been focused on the specifics we have been looking for. By the time they put it all together, everyone will be gone and there will be no way to prove what happened."

Clint understood. He knew from his past that the intel

world would often describe a person as being "linked" to the murders of several people. The key word being linked, meaning we know it, but we can't prove it. Without proof, most western nations were hesitant to take positive action.

"Your target remains Agape, but I wouldn't lose much sleep over any collateral. These are bad people. They won't be taking the two women back to wherever to teach high school science."

"I know."

"But, Clint, don't get yourself killed. Once your target is down, get yourself out of there. You can't save everybody."

"I need to go, Buzz. It will take me a few minutes to get set up."

"Good luck," Buzz said and ended the call.

Nothing had driven by while Clint was on the phone. He wondered if his target had already arrived and was waiting near the pier. He steered the motorcycle back onto the road and coasted down the hill into the town. He passed the split in the road where he believed the right fork took trucks or other vehicles around the town to the pier. The town had few other side streets. All the buildings were dark, and he saw no one. As he approached the edge of the town that bumped against the shoreline, he turned onto the street toward the pier. He went to the last building on the street before the road continued out into the open. He parked the motorcycle in an alley between what looked like a supply store for fishermen and a pub.

He walked to the back of the store and studied the pier and the area around it. He saw no people and no vehicles. The boat looked as though it had stopped a half mile offshore. He checked the time and saw that it was sixteen minutes until two.

He figured the rendezvous time would be on the hour. That gave him ten to twelve minutes to find a place to hide, unless Agape and crew arrived early.

Clint walked out into the open field toward the pier. The road had been built up four or five feet higher than sea level, so he kept the road to his left between him and boat. A single lamp on a wooden pole at the entrance to the pier provided a little light to the immediate surroundings. As he approached, he saw the area around the entrance to the pier cluttered with numerous items: empty wooden pallets, old netting, old rope wound up in rolls, two large trash containers, a fuel pump and long fueling hose, and an old, worn-down outhouse.

Concealment would not be a problem, but picking the best place might be. He could not be sure which approach they would use to get to the pier. He had to be sure his concealment wouldn't be compromised by vehicle headlights coming from either direction.

It was a lesson well learned. He lost a friend in Afghanistan when an enemy unit arrived via a different trail than they had expected and caught his friend's army element off guard. In life and death situations, one should never assume anything. It only takes one mistake to cost you your life.

Besides concealment, he had to consider egress. What if he was seriously outgunned and had to leave. The more he studied the area, the more he wished he did have that sniper rifle. An open field ran for a hundred yards in every direction. He liked the area on the other side of the road that circumvented the town. It was darker. A mix of netting and rope piled three feet high and about ten feet wide would give him plenty of room to hide and maneuver behind.

Clint crossed the road, trying to look as casual as he could. He didn't think anyone on the boat would be paying too much attention to the area until the car or whatever came with the two women. He reached the bundle of netting and inspected it. He liked its proximity to the pier and the cover it would give him, but it was too close to the outhouse. Someone walking to or from it would see him. He moved to the outhouse. No good, he thought. Even a .22 caliber round would go right through its thin aluminum walls.

He decided to head back to the motorcycle. It made more sense to try to accomplish his mission as his target drove back to the main highway. As luck would have it, the headlights of two vehicles rounding a bend on the road around the town forced him to duck behind the outhouse. He immediately crouched low to the ground, staying close to the outhouse. The few tall weeds provided minimal concealment. While he was now out of view from anyone in the cars, someone on the boat might be able to see him.

Too late to go anywhere now, he thought.

Clint heard the boat's motor rev up, and it resumed its approach. Fortunately, the closer it got, the more cover the outhouse provided. He remained where he was until he heard the two vehicles stop. He did not hear any car doors opening.

They're waiting for the boat, Clint thought. He stood up but stayed behind the outhouse. After a few minutes, he could hear the boat's engine go in reverse as the boat eased against the pier. Car doors opened, and he could hear men talking in Greek. Someone shouted a greeting from the boat.

Clint peeked around the shady side of the outhouse. He saw a van. A driver sat inside, but the doors and the back of the van were still closed. Ahead of it, two men stood outside a black sedan. Thanks to the light from the pole, he could tell the man closest to him was Agape. He could see no one else in the car.

His target was barely in range. It would have to be a good shot, but he had made such shots before. Exposing himself now, however, would be foolish. He needed to wait for a better opportunity.

Chapter 44

"We're slowing down," Kim said.

Melody remained quiet. Kim's remark didn't need an answer. They had their plan, as simple as it might be. When someone opened the van's doors they would attack. Kicking, head butting, biting, whatever it took to be able to run away. She knew they had little chance that their plan would work, but they had to do something.

She could feel the van turn off the road they had been on for at least an hour. It came to a brief stop before turning left. The van accelerated but to a much slower speed than before. The road had more bumps than the highway. Before long they slowed again and made a right turn.

"We must be getting close," Kim said.

"Yes." Melody responded this time. "Are you ready?"

"As ready as I can be."

Melody felt the way Kim sounded. She had little confidence their plan would work. She forced herself to fight the urge to simply give up. How could this be happening to them? Hadn't they suffered enough.

The van slowed to a crawl, and she could hear the crunch of sand on the road beneath the tires. The van stopped but nothing happened.

"Our driver is staying in the van," Kim finally said. "Think they are going to load us on a ferry?"

Melody thought Kim's running commentary was unnecessary, but could they be waiting to get on a ferry? That was not something she had ever considered.

"I can't imagine they would allow us to go on board a ferry without first drugging us. We can make a lot of noise shouting. That would alert someone. Maybe we ought to start screaming," Melody said.

"Wait a second," Kim said. "I hear someone talking."

Melody had not heard anyone. She listened and heard what sounded like two men talking in the distance. They stopped talking, and it surprised her when just a few seconds later, she heard someone nearby talking to the driver. The voice made her tremble. She recognized it as the voice of the man who had ordered the murder of Professor Dean, the man who had assaulted her. Foolishly, she had let herself hope he hadn't come with them.

"That's that bastard," Kim said.

"Yes, I want to kill him."

Although the darkness inside of the van prevented Melody from seeing her, Kim nodded. "I want to kill him, too. If we can't escape, let's at least kill the bastard."

The discussion at the driver's window stopped. Melody expected the van's back door to open, but it didn't.

A minute later she could hear more people talking in the distance.

"What's going on?" Kim asked.

"I don't know," Melody said, trying to keep the irritation out of her voice. She knew it was natural for Kim to react to the situation by talking, but she was the opposite. She didn't want to talk or to have to think of things to say. She wanted it to be quiet, so she could think.

Melody heard a light rain start to fall on the van's roof. She prayed for a violent storm, anything that might throw her abductor's plans awry. She prayed for a miracle.

"It's hard to hear them now. Not sure if it's the rain or if they've stopped talking. Maybe they've left us here to be discovered by someone, or to die in this van," Kim said.

"If they abandon us here, we will discover a way to escape. This van cannot be impenetrable."

Nothing happened in the next two minutes. They sat in silent anticipation. The sound of the driver's door opening and then closing finally broke the silence. To Melody's relief, Kim didn't say anything.

"What time do you think it is?" Melody asked after another minute of nothing breaking the silence but the light patter of rain on the roof.

"I have no idea. Night time I would think. They woke me up, but they could have been having us sleep during the day and working at night. Do you really think the guys are dead? I can't get my mind around it."

"I can't get my mind around any of this."

"I wish it was lighter in here. This darkness is getting to me," Kim said.

They sat in silence for another two to three minutes.

"Someone said something," Kim said. "It sounded like a cough."

"Shh," Melody hushed her. She hadn't heard anything, but she was tired of Kim reporting everything she heard.

Melody felt a slight shake of the van, like something pushed or bumped against it. She didn't hear anything. The strain of their situation grew on her. She started to think if she didn't scream, she was going to explode.

As if her feeling was mutual, Kim leaned closer to Melody and managed to reach out and gently took hold of Melody's arm. Despite her hands being tied behind her, she stretched and put her hand over Kim's. A moment later she heard someone say something.

"That sounded like someone was cussing," Kim said.

A few seconds later the driver's door opened, and the driver got back into the van.

Chapter 45

Clint didn't like the odds. He counted five men and had to consider they each carried a gun of some sort. He didn't see any, and that was good, but he couldn't count out a stray assault rifle in one or both of the vehicles. Additionally, more men and weapons had to be on the boat.

Rain started to fall. Agape and one of the men who walked down the pier from the boat got into the back of the dark sedan. The sedan's driver stayed outside, so they were likely discussing business or something else private. The second man from the boat stood off to the side.

Clint looked around the other corner of the outhouse and saw that the other man he had seen on the deck of the boat had disappeared. The steady, light rain may have driven him and any others inside. When the shooting started, they wouldn't stay inside.

He heard a car door close and saw the driver of the van round the front of the van and start walking his way. Must need to use the outhouse, he thought. Clint ran a dozen scenarios through his head before the man opened the door unaware of Clint's presence a few feet away. The door swung open in a way that blocked the view of the van and car. The rest of the outhouse blocked the view from the boat.

As the man stepped to enter, Clint came around the corner. The man, startled, reached for a pistol tucked into the front of his pants. Clint fired two rounds into his chest. The man staggered backwards against the door, but Clint grabbed him and pushed him inside. The small space inside made it awkward, but Clint guided the man's collapse. Now dead, he ended up sitting on the wooden bench above the cut-out hole and slumped against the back wall.

"Perfect," Clint said to himself. He removed the man's brown jacket and put it on over his own. The man was heavy set, so other than the sleeves being short, the jacket fit well enough to be partially zipped up. He needed to have the others think that he was the van's driver returning from the outhouse. He only needed to fool them until he got close. The man would be expected to be inside for about a minute. Clint didn't think anyone would have heard the muffled sounds of the two shots.

While Clint waited, he heard the crunching of sand and dirt as someone approached. A man rapped on the door and called out a name. After only a few seconds, the man rapped again on the door and pulled it open. He started to say something but saw Clint. His first reaction, like the man before him, was to reach for a pistol in his coat pocket, partially pulling it out.

Clint fired once and grabbed the man, pulling him into the outhouse. He would normally fire a second shot, but he knew his first round hit the man in his heart. The man went limp before he was totally in the cramped space of the outhouse. Clint caught him as he started to fall.

He had to struggle with this second man. Between the man's dead weight and the lack of room, it took all Clint's strength to force him onto the bench next to first man.

Other than a set of keys in the first man's pocket, neither man had anything else in their pockets. Two down, three to go, Clint would love to have one more come to the outhouse, but he knew he would soon be out of time. He also didn't want to be trapped inside the outhouse. He picked up the second man's pistol that had fallen to the floor. Thankfully, the floor was dry.

He put the smallish, Sig Sauer pistol in the pocket of the outer coat he now wore. He wouldn't use it, unless he had to. Silence was his friend, but he had used a lot of his ammunition tonight. He knew he didn't have much to spare.

Clint adjusted the Covid mask and pulled his cap lower over his forehead. He left the outhouse and walked casually toward the van. He kept himself bent over, like someone might to keep the rain out of his face.

The driver of the sedan leaned against the front of the van, smoking and looking off at the town. The other two still sat in the car that was parked in front of and off to the side of the van. No one was out on the deck of the boat.

The driver glanced at Clint as he approached, but didn't realize who it wasn't until too late. He drew his pistol faster than Clint anticipated, but not fast enough. Only ten feet separated the two when Clint fired two rounds into his chest. He collapsed against the hood of the van before sliding to the ground with his back still against the vehicle. A moment later, he fell sideways from his sitting position, and his face splashed into a small puddle.

Clint immediately walked to the sedan. He knew there might still be a hitch if the vehicle had been armored against small caliber weapons and the doors were locked. Unlikely, he knew, and locked doors by themselves would not be a problem.

He opened the back passenger door of the sedan. Both men inside shouted out in anger, but they became silent when they realized the intruder wasn't one of their employees. They scrambled for their own weapons, but Clint didn't give them enough time.

After he verified both had died or would be soon, Clint took a picture of each man to send them to Section. He also took their cell phones and some cash from Agape's wallet. He hadn't taken pictures of the three other men at the scene, because he didn't have time. He still didn't, so he hurried to the van and climbed into the driver's seat. A wall separated the cab from the back of the van.

The boat still sat at the end of the pier. Clint figured if anyone aboard the boat had noticed something, they would at least be shouting to their compatriots on shore. He knew it was time to leave.

The van was an older one. He fished out the keys he had taken from the man's pocket in the outhouse, finding the one that fit into the ignition switch. He started the van's engine and drove it the short distance to the edge of town. He parked in front of the bait shop.

"Are you two alright?"

Chapter 46

"We're moving again," Kim said.

"I hate this. I wish we knew what was going on," Melody said.

"Why were we stopped so long?"

"At least we're safe in the van. It's when we're stopped that I worry about."

"What if they don't plan on selling us. What if they are going to kill us. They don't ever have to let out us out of the van," Kim said.

Melody started to say that they had already discussed that, but the van came to a stop. She tensed and felt Kim do the same.

"Are you two alright?" a man asked.

The man spoke English. Melody didn't recognize the voice. A flood of emotions ran through her. She couldn't answer.

"Help us!" Kim shouted.

"I will. I'm going to open the back of the van, but please don't scream. If we want to escape, we'll need to do it silently," the man said.

Melody whispered, "Rescue." She couldn't say more, she felt dizzy. She fought to stay focused. Had someone really come to rescue them? It had been so long. She had given up hope. What if this was just a sadistic joke. She heard Kim start to cry.

She recognized the sound of someone fumbling with keys, trying to unlock the van's back door. Finally, the lock gave, and a man pulled the door open. Dim light penetrated the inside of the van. She sensed, rather than saw, Kim scoot backwards away from the door. She knew why. The man outside was dressed in black, wore a dark mask like the ones people wore during Covid, and had a stocking cap pulled down to his eyes. More importantly, he held a gun in his right hand aimed at the interior of the cabin.

Unlike Kim, she wasn't intimidated by his appearance. In her dreams, her hopes, her prayers, she fantasized a super hero coming to her rescue. All her superheroes wore masks. They didn't want to be recognized, and they all carried weapons. She was a realist, and a calmness returned to her.

"Can you walk?" he asked.

"Yes," Melody said.

"Better yet, can you drive?"

"Yes,"

"Who are you?" Kim asked.

"We don't need to know," Melody said.

The man looked at Melody and said, "Thanks."

"You need to call the police," Kim said.

"No need for that right now. The best thing for you to do is drive this van out of here and head to Athens. Here are the keys."

"What happened to the men who had us. I don't understand," Kim said.

"They won't bother you anymore, but I don't know about the others."

"The others?" Melody asked.

"The few still on the boat. They were to be your new owners. I don't think they noticed our departure, but you don't have much time."

"But how?" Kim asked.

"How about the two men who were prisoners with us?" Melody asked before their rescuer could answer Kim's question.

"They are safe. Drive this van--"

"They're alive!" Kim interrupted.

"Yes, drive this van straight ahead to the main road, about a hundred yards in that direction. You can't miss it. Then take that road to the left through the town to the highway. It's only a mile and a half. You can't miss the highway either. Turn left and take it all the way to Athens. The gas tank is almost full."

"Shouldn't we call the police?" Kim asked.

"No, it's not safe to wait around here. Besides, I can't be found here. I'm not supposed to be here. Do me one favor. Don't describe me too well."

"Can we say a woman rescued us?" Melody asked.

"Of course. Please just agree on your description of me as a woman before you talk to anyone, and then stick to it. The two men have also agreed to that, but there is no need for the four of you to describe the same person."

"Can we first call our family?" Kim asked.

"I left you two cell phones and a wad of cash up front in the van. Their owners have no need of them anymore. You can call whomever you want once you're on the road."

"Will we see you again?" Melody asked.

"I hope you won't need to."

"I can't believe this is happening," Kim said.

"With the exception of your description of me, tell the authorities the truth about everything. Everything. Do we have a deal?"

"Yes," both women said.

"You'll need to free us from these ties," Melody said and turned to show him her wrists.

"Come closer," he said, and cut the ties with a knife he pulled out of his pocket. He gave Kim the keys.

"No sidekick?" Melody asked while he cut her ties.

"Yes, but he's working remote." He grinned at her. He had looked confused at first, and then he seemed to understand.

"Thank you," Melody said.

"Don't speed, but you better get going right now. I don't know if the men who had you have other friends in this small town," the man said.

"Tell me for sure, they're dead. All the men who brought us here are dead, right?" Kim asked. Melody could sense the emotion in her voice.

"Yes, they're dead. You're safe." He walked down the alley next to them and disappeared.

"Let's move," Melody said. For the first time that night, she saw the bruising on Kim's face and understood what likely happened to her.

They both rushed around to the front of the van.

"Let me drive. I've been driving in Europe all my life," Kim said.

Without any hesitation, Kim started the van and drove them through the small town and out to the highway.

Melody checked out the two phones. They seemed to be in working order. She counted three hundred and twelve euros in the stash of cash. She also inspected an old brown coat that was on the floor in front of the passenger seat.

"This might keep one of us warm – yuck!" She saw the two bullet holes and found blood on the inside of the coat.

"What was it?" Kim asked.

"A coat. I believe it belonged to one of the men who had us. It has two holes that I think are bullet holes through it. It also has some blood on it."

"I might want it as a souvenir."

"You can have it."

"Traffic is light. That's good. Does this thing have a clock in it? We should have asked that man what time it was."

"You mean that woman?" Melody said and smiled.

"Yes, that woman. We should have also asked him what day it was."

"Hold on, the phones should tell us." Melody read off the date and the time.

Both women remained silent for a few seconds.

"It's hard to believe. I don't know if I thought we were there longer, or if I'm surprised how long we were there. That's how mixed up I was, and I guess still am," Kim said.

"Me, too. I kept wishing it was all a bad dream. Now I'm afraid that this is a dream, and in a minute, I'll wake up and find myself back in that horrible place."

"Don't even say that. Call someone, anyone. Tell them we're free. Tell them we're heading to Athens, and we need help getting to the Austrian and US Embassies."

Chapter 47

Clint heard the van leave before he reached the motorcycle. They had already turned onto the city's main street by the time he drove onto the side road. He drove the motorcycle at a jogger's pace. At this slow speed the small engine made very little noise. He rounded the corner onto the main street to head out of town and saw the van's taillights a half a mile away. He maintained his slow speed until he hit the edge of town. He could no longer see the van. He thought he had stayed far enough behind the van to have not been seen.

Once on the highway, he traveled straight back to the hotel in Thessaloniki. At nearly four thirty in the morning, the city was still asleep. The hotel clerk gave him a half wave and went back to fiddling with his phone. For his part, Clint tried to put a little stagger in his walk, so the clerk would think he had been drinking.

He had expected a call from Buzz or Deer once he arrived at the hotel, but none had come. He showered and went to bed. He would contact them in the morning. He fell asleep, acknowledging he had some psychological issues. He had killed around a dozen people that day and felt no remorse. Why was that, he wondered, but he fell asleep before he paid it much thought.

The sound of his phone pulled him out of a deep sleep. Sunshine crept in from around the corners of the curtains. He sat up, rubbed his eyes, and looked at his phone.

"Good morning. I'm assuming you're okay," Buzz said.

"Yes." Clint scratched his nose and blinked a few times.

"Can you make the noon ferry to Athens?"

Clint looked at the time and saw that gave him two hours. "I should be able to. Why the rush?"

"She wants to get you out of there ASAP and as discreetly as possible."

"Has it started getting hot here?"

"Not yet, but it will. The world is aware that the four scientists are free. Everyone now knows they had been held in Thessaloniki. Well, it hasn't hit the press yet, but that's only a matter of time. The crazy thing is that no one has located any of the bodies yet."

"Aren't the scientists talking?"

"Yes, but none of them have any real idea where they were at any point of their captivity. The two men could only say they were taken a few miles up the coast from Thessaloniki, and the women couldn't even narrow it down that much."

"The town folk must have found and reported the bodies by now," Clint said.

"Not a peep. We find that very interesting, too. Deer's guess is that the people in that town don't want anyone to know about what happened there."

"Why would they want to keep it a secret?"

"They might be afraid Agape's friends may blame everything on them, or they might not want the national police to scrutinize their little town. A lot of things may have made their way in and out of Greece through their little harbor without the authorities' knowledge. At this point, we have no way of really knowing."

"Interesting."

"We agree. So far, the scientists have done a good job at misleading everyone. The two women insist a woman rescued them, and the two men have described you as being about four inches shorter than you are. All four said their rescuer wore a mask, had a cap pulled down to just above their eyes, wore dark clothes, and spoke English."

"Good."

"We think so, too. By the way, the man with Agape was a bad character, too. He was a lieutenant, for lack of a better word, in a rather nasty North African cartel. This cartel of his is deeply involved in all sorts of bad behavior. Human trafficking being one of them. Assassination being another." Buzz said.

"Could they have been behind the drone attacks?"

"More than likely, they were involved in some way. What you need to know is that there is a growing relationship among several of the world's criminal cartels. The internet has made it easier for them to interact and deconflict issues. It's entirely possible this cartel was serving as a middle man between Agape and anyone who wanted to make use of his drones."

"Looks like you have a whole new area to look into." He didn't agree with Buzz that he needed to know about the internet and the world getting more dangerous. The world had always been a dangerous place.

"I will. It's fascinating. It's like a jigsaw puzzle. Oh, by the way, I just need to verify it for the boss, but you did get rid of the pistol already. Right?"

"Yes. It's safely gone."

"Good. We'll text you with the latest before your ferry leaves."

The call ended, and Clint started packing. He had disassembled the Beretta the night before, while waiting for the van to get far enough ahead of him. He had tossed the barrel by itself into the first good size river he crossed on the way to the hotel and the rest of the pistol into the second. He had tossed the Sig Sauer he had picked up off the floor of the outhouse into the car next to Agape before he left them.

Deer called him as the ferry started to leave. She told him that nothing had changed. The authorities had still not been able to locate the two sites. She felt the local police in Thessaloniki might be dragging their feet to let what remained of Agape's empire cover their tracks. The Greek national police had sent a team to the city. Once it arrived, the city police would likely announce they had discovered the site.

Clint figured she was right. The local police didn't know Agape was dead. They wouldn't move too fast. Over time, the word would get out, and there would be a major power struggle in the city, perhaps throughout the country. If the police were smart, they would get a jump on that and round up all Agape's known associates.

The ferry arrived in Athens in the evening. Section had booked him for one night back into the Marriot. That pleased him as he would like to see Cher again. Unfortunately, that never happened. He walked to the restaurant and discovered that Cher and her mother had gone to visit an aunt in a small city a couple hours north of Athens. They wouldn't be returning until late the next day. Clint had tickets to fly to Madrid in the early afternoon. He left a message for her saying goodbye again.

He did see Tish the next morning. She brought him coffee and a croissant before he could ask for anything.

"I'm happy to see you again. How'd you bruise that handsome face of yours?" Tish asked.

Clint had noticed the slight swelling and discoloration the previous morning before he got on the ferry. He wore a Covid mask while getting on the ferry. The bruising was slight, but he worried about security cameras at the port. Once the ferry set sail, he kept to quiet areas on the ship but didn't continue to wear the mask.

"Long story, but it's nothing." They talked for a few minutes more before a restaurant manager called Tish away.

He arrived in Madrid in the late afternoon, and as in Athens, Section booked him into the same hotel he had stayed in before. Buzz called him after he was in his room for the night.

"They finally located the place where the two men were taken. The Greek authorities are quite riled up about it. I'm not sure if they were more embarrassed that the scientists were kept under their noses in Greece, or the fact that someone killed a half dozen of their citizens without giving them any heads-up."

"Not very good citizens, I'd say."

"No not at all. The guy Eddy, and no one seems to know his full name or much more about him other than he was a well-known vicious thug, seems to have had quite the reputation. I think most of the city police force were terrified of him."

"He nearly killed me."

"I wouldn't have liked that."

Clint had to smile at his remark.

"In a smart political move, our Ambassador took it upon himself to publicly thank the Greek government for their assistance in rescuing the scientists," Buzz said.

"Why would he do that?"

"Not sure. Deer thinks that he probably thought that the rescue was a sanctioned US rescue and tried to soothe the Greeks feelings. Either way, it may preclude the Greeks from complaining much more. The Austrian and Japanese ambassadors piggy-backed and also thanked the Greek government."

"Interesting, and how are the scientists?"

"Free and very happy to be so. They haven't said much publicly yet. News of Dean's death has dampened the celebrations so far."

"The scientists have confirmed that they were forced to provide technical recommendations to improve a drone's performance, but they never saw a drone and were not sure what drone they were enhancing. They also didn't know what or who the targets were. However, they had to watch one video of the general killed in Africa. All but Dr. Mose also watched their captors murder Henry Dean. Their stories are consistent with each other."

Before disconnecting, Buzz said Deer wanted him to stay in Madrid for a week or so. They would continue to monitor the situation. This time, they didn't have to remind him to keep a low profile.

The next morning, he ran into Steffi at the café on the Plaza Major. They picked up their relationship like they had just seen each other the day before. Other than one question about Clint's bruised face, neither asked any questions or needed any explanation as to what they had done during their absence. While Clint did wonder if Steffi's world was as mysterious as his, he didn't care. For two days, they spent a lot of time together at the café chatting about a variety of topics. On the morning of the third day, they agreed to take a four-day road trip around Spain. He would drive and she would navigate. It was a very nice week.

He hadn't thought about his car until he was on his flight back to Houston. Earlier, Buzz had said something about finding him a new one. He guessed that Buzz had been teasing him, but a text from him just before the plane took off had him wondering.

"Clint, we had to move your car. We'll give you an update when you land," the text said.

Clint grinned and closed his eyes. It would be a long flight.

Chapter 48

Efran ended the telephone call with his close friend. He had only been in Venice a day. He had to sit down on the plastic chair on the hotel room's small balcony. He couldn't believe it. He had heard the news of the scientists' escape on the television that morning. He didn't understand the Italian language, but the news was easy enough to understand. They had been rescued. The happiness that erupted within him surprised him.

Later, in the afternoon Efran worked up the courage to call his close friend. This friend was one of a few who knew he was an employee, an unhappy employee, of that monster, Sonder Agape. His friend knew no details of Efran's job, except that he repaired a few things for Agape. Efran knew he suspected a lot more. Everyone in the region knew of Agape's brutal reputation. Yet his friend did not blame Efran. People did what Agape told them to do.

His friend told him the word on the street was that Agape was missing, believed to be dead, and that Eddy's body had been found, along with several of Agape's gang of murderers. No details had been made public, but this was a story that one couldn't keep a lid on in Thessaloniki.

Efran worried his connection with Agape may lead the police to him. His concern, however, was insignificant compared to his sense of relief, of freedom. He called his wife to the balcony. When she came, she saw he was crying.

"What's wrong?" she asked and hugged him.

"Nothing, nothing. They are happy tears. Everything is good. Did you see?"

"See what?" Efran knew she cared little for the news.

"The scientists are free," he said.

She looked at him, bewildered. He had never mentioned the scientists to her.

"We are free, too, my love. We are, too."

Title: *The Attack*™
Author: Bob Doerr
Publisher: TotalRecall Publications, Inc.
Paper Back: ISBN: 9781590951460
Book: ISBN: 9781590951477
Number of pages in the finished book:
Publication Date: 2014

A terrorist team has just set off four explosive devices in an international airport close to New York City. The leader of the terrorists, Ahmad Khalin, survives the attack and plans to attack a second U.S. airport within the month. As Khalin makes his escape from the New York area he is involved in a shooting in Connecticut. Clint Smith, a U.S. government agent assigned to an ultra-secret agency, is at a restaurant across the street when the shooting occurs. He responds to the scene to see if he can help, but Khalin is gone. On a hunch, Teresa Deer, Smith's boss, sends Smith after Khalin. Smith's pursuit takes him to Bar Harbor, Maine; Wiesbaden, Germany; the Costa Brava, Spain; Northern Scotland; Lake of the Woods, Ontario, Canada; and finally into Saskatchewan, Canada, where the final confrontation takes place. Throughout the pursuit, a number of interesting characters add to the subplots and try to survive their involvement in the chase.

***A Clint Smith Thriller*™**

Title: *The Group*™
Author: Bob Doerr
Publisher: TotalRecall Publications, Inc.
Paper Back: ISBN: 9781590955697
eBook: ISBN: 9781590955703
Number of pages in the finished book: 288
Publication Date: 2016

A fast-moving international thriller that pits a lone government operative, known as a hunter, against an unknown group of assassins who pose a worldwide threat.

Someone is killing off the world's rich and famous. The murders are sophisticated, requiring precision and skill. The international community is in an uproar but has no leads in its attempt to find the assassins. The victims were members of the Bilderberg Group, an international, loose knit group of the uber rich that meet annually. While the attacks have not had a direct impact on the U.S., Theresa Deer, Director of the Special Section, a small unit whose existence is known by only a handful in the U.S. government, sees this new age League of Assassins as a national threat. She sends her hunters out. Clint Smith finds their trail Switzerland where his discovery almost leads to his own death. The hunt leads him to Mallorca, Spain, where he witnesses a helicopter attack on a villa where a number of attendees from the Bilderberg conference were holding a follow-on meeting of their own. Smith picks up the trail a couple weeks later in Las Vegas, NV, and in his hunt finds out that he is no longer the hunter. He has become the prey.

***A Clint Smith Thriller*™**

Title: *The Assassins*™
Author: Bob Doerr
Publisher: TotalRecall Publications, Inc.
Paper Back: ISBN: 9781590951965
eBook: ISBN: 9781590951972
Number of pages in the finished book: 242
Publication Date: 2018

A disputed election has divided the nation, and a handful of senior government officials have conspired to have the North Koreans assassinate the President of the United States. Believing the assassination attempt to be only days away, Theresa Deer, Director of the Special Section, a small unit whose existence is known by only a few in the U.S. government, is tasked to interdict the man intent on providing the North Koreans vital information about the president's itinerary for his visit to South Korea. While Deer succeeds in her mission, she is severely injured and finds herself being hunted by the North Korean assassins. Clint Smith is sent to Korea to help Deer get back to the U.S. and finds himself caught in a deadly game of cat and mouse with the North Koreans. With no one in the U.S. government to turn to for help, and the South Koreans now also hunting them, getting out of South Korea alive is looking unlikely.

***A Clint Smith Thriller*™**

Title: *The Treasure*™
Author: Bob Doerr
Publisher: TotalRecall Publications, Inc.
Paper Back: ISBN: 9781648830846
eBook: ISBN: 9781648830853
Number of pages in the finished book: 252
Publication Date: 2021

The Treasure is the fourth book in the Clint Smith thriller series. After a successful mission in South America, Clint heads to Las Vegas on vacation and to dig up a stagecoach strong box he had found in the desert earlier but had not opened. Upon inspection, he finds some old gold coins in mint condition and some well-preserved documents. He gives the contents of the strong box to a lawyer to find buyers. One of the documents, unfortunately, creates a maelstrom of violence and murder, and puts Clint squarely in the cross hairs of some Chinese assassins. Clint leaves Las Vegas to keep out of the spotlight, only to find himself going to Alaska in an attempt to rescue a female police officer who had been assigned to protect him in Las Vegas.

A Clint Smith Thriller™

Titles by Bob Doerr

Mystery Detective Suspense Thrillers

Dead Men Can Kill

Cold Winters Kill

Another Colorado Kill

Loose Ends Kill

No One Else To Kill

Caffeine Can Kill

Greed Can Kill

Honeymoons Can Kill

Double Bogeys Can Kill

Action Adventure Series

The Attack

The Group

The Assassins

The Treasure

The Scientists

Mouse Gate Series

The Enchanted Coin

The Rescue of Vincent

The Magic of Vex

Stranded in Space

Author Bob Doerr Uses his special knowledge to provide
authentic details in his novels about how
law enforcement agencies do their work.
For a complete list of books by Bob Doerr,
a preview of upcoming titles and more
visit his website.

www.bobdoerr.com

Locate Bob on Facebook and
let him know how you like his books.

www.ingramcontent.com/pod-product-compliance
Lightning Source LLC
Chambersburg PA
CBHW070835020826
48982CB00019B/1251/J

* 9 7 8 1 6 4 8 8 3 3 1 2 0 *